CARNIVAL FARM

LISA JACOB

DEDICATION

To Don, who would have read this book.

1

S EAGN CONWAY GAZED INTO THE SAD BROWN EYES of the cow leaning heavily against the iron gate in front of her. She scratched the cow under its chin. The cow tried to lick her hand.

Seagn sighed, looked out at the twenty assorted farm animals in the pen. Crowded under a single ten-foot long tent, with one rusted barrel of water between shared between them all, it was no wonder everyone went straight into the carnival and didn't even bother to stop to see the farm animals. They looked worn, sick, or old.

Seeing them like this broke her heart.

Seagn caught the eye of the nearest person wearing a "Rockwell Carnival" t-shirt. "You know who owns these animals?"

"Fatsy?" The man gave her a grin, revealing three missing teeth and the remainder were all black. "He's with Webby."

"Where?"

The man pointed with a wavering cigarette. "The RV over there."

At the edge of the carnival, parked between a couple of trailers, sat an RV. Three people sat at a table under the shade of its awning.

In a fury, she pushed through and dodged groups of people to get to the RV. It was only five years after the Pandemic, and people were still leery of her pushing them around, coming within a six-foot distance.

Two large men and an equally large woman sat precariously on large folding chairs, each drinking cans of Coors Lite.

"Who's Fatsy?" she demanded.

"Who're you?" the larger of the two large men snapped at her in the same tone.

"I'm Dr. Shaun Conway. I'm a vet."

"Fuck," Fatsy set down his beer. "They all got their rabies shots."

Seagn put her hand on her hip, a sure sign that a tirade was coming soon. "Those animals yours?"

"Yeah."

"I want to examine them."

"You can see 'em through the fence, can't you?"

"They're under duress."

"They're under the tent."

"Fatsy," said the woman. "Don't give the doctor a hard time." She smiled, although it was forced, at Seagn. "We have all the necessary papers to display these farm animals."

"They're sick. Depressed."

Fatsy snorted.

"What do you suggest? We send the clowns over to entertain them?" This from the other large man, obviously "Webby".

"As a matter of fact, I do have a few suggestions," she said, going to lean on the precarious table, then stepping back when it jostled the cans of beer. "How much to buy the animals from you?"

Fatsy and Webby blinked.

"They're not for sale," said the woman.

"Now, hold on —" began Webby.

"No," said Seagn. "*You* hold on. I want control of those animals, and I'll bring them up to snuff. Healthy, and even give pony rides on that little Shetland you have there. I'll give people a reason to come to your carnival, to see beautiful specimens of farm life in the middle of the city. Sell them to me."

"Eight thousand dollars."

The woman glared at Webby.

Seagn rocked. It was a hefty amount. "Including the trailer and tent, all the trappings it has."

"Agreed," said Webby. "If you can do what you say, then it'll be worth it. You gotta buy your own feed, though."

Now it was her turn to blink. That was going to cost a lot, especially the healthy kind of feed she had in mind. "I accept that. Draw up a contract." She looked to Fatsy. "Got any problems with that?"

Fatsy struggled out of the chair, as if it had molded itself around him. It came up when he stood and he had to push the arms of the chair off his hips to get clear. "Where'm I gonna go? All my crap's in the truck."

"I don't care," Seagn said. "You didn't care about the animals, why should I care about you?"

Fatsy looked as Webby went into the RV. Fatsy then looked at Seagn. Her fury eased somewhat at seeing Fatsy's helpless face, but this man abused these animals. She knew it, and she wasn't about to let him get off scot-free. He seemed the type to have a Plan B for himself, anyway.

She wasn't worried about the eight grand. She had more than enough saved up from the sale of her parents' house a few years ago when she started her job at the Central Avenue Vet. Five years later, she was bored to tears with dogs and cats and the every-once-in-a-while rabbit. Farm animals were not her specialty, but she had the Internet.

The carnival advertised that it was going to be in town for the weekend, so she had a lot of work to do. Clean up the apartment, settle her debts, and first: quit her job.

She smiled. Hailey was going to love that.

•　　　•　　　•

"No notice?"

Seagn packed her few personal belongings from their shared desk. She checked the computer, but nothing personal was on it. Maybe some pictures, but not much.

Hailey yanked on the end of her own ponytail.

"You're — You're just … leaving?"

"Yes. You'll be fine. In fact, you can hire that guy who worked here this winter."

Hailey exhaled. Seagn tried not to grin. Hailey, younger than Seagn by three years, never let her forget who the owner and boss of the place was. Since the owners changed hands last year and Hailey was in charge, it had been a crappy job. Seagn had been looking for a way out.

God (or Whoever) had seen fit to present her with this opportunity: to do what she loved with a whole new set of exotic-to-her animals.

Seagn straightened with the box full of her stuff. "So there it is."

Hailey again tugged her pony tail.

"Goodbye," Seagn said, while she finally grinned.

She used her hip to push open the half-door leading out of the doctors' office. The rest of the staff craned their necks to see where she was going. Some rose from their chairs to watch her walk out. Seagn said nothing to the receptionists or the patients in the waiting room.

She put her items in her ancient yellow VW's "trunk", which was the front of the car. After slamming down the hood, she glanced back at the clinic's windows. No one had gathered to see her off.

Seagn frowned. If they didn't need her, she didn't need them. She got into her car and drove to the animal shelter on the outskirts of the town of Salem.

Decorated throughout the year with black cats and pumpkins, the Town of Salem's shelter was adorned in perpetual

Halloween mode. But then, that was the town for most of the year. After all, Salem had a reputation to keep up.

The dogs were out in the spring weather, and the parking lot had only a few cars in it. There were hardly any adopted dogs from the shelter this past year, but most of the ones that passed through her clinic were for the basics of spay/neuter, heartworm, and some with broken bones. Kristen White, one of the Animal Control Officers of Salem, usually presented Seagn with the complicated cases.

"Doc Shaun," called the receptionist with a wave and a smile.

"Hiya. Is Kristen here?"

"In the back. She just got a new bully, and you know how she is with getting them acclimated."

Treats and cuddles, Seagn thought. Unless they were stressed, then it was treats tossed to those fighting-breed dogs from a distance.

She walked past the receptionist's area through to the back office and found Kristen with a ragged bully dog that looked like he had seen better days. He wagged his tail at her approach, though.

Kristen noticed her. "Hey, Doc."

"Hiya. Who's this?"

"Don't know. He was abandoned in the dog park. Probably a fighter."

Seagn could tell by the scars on the dog's haunches that Kristen's guess was probably right. But he was still wagging his tail and bumping up against Seagn to be pet.

"You got him calmed down."

"Nothing a little trust can't do. Speaking of which, what are you doing here?"

"I'm leaving the practice."

Kristen sighed. "It took you long enough. Are you going into your own clinic?"

"No, I'm joining the circus."

Kristen stopped playing with the dog and gave her a sidelong glance. "You're not serious."

"I'm dead serious. Have you seen the animals in the pens over at the carnival nearby? They're in horrible condition."

"You're going to save them?"

"Every one of them, and turn it into a functioning petting zoo."

Kristen looked forlorn.

"Hey, the city still has an agreement with the practice," Seagn reassured her.

"For how long? We come in with the complicated cases and you take care of them for free or near free. Hailey isn't going to do that for long."

Seagn shook her head. "The animals need me more than Hailey does."

Kristen absently stroked the new bully, who seemed to sense the sadness in the room.

"I'll probably be back in the winter, unless they go south."

"You don't know?"

Seagn shrugged. "It was an impulse thing."

Kristen laughed. "You always do that."

"It seemed like a good idea at the time," she mused. "You know how I hate to see animals suffering."

"It's part of your charm."

Kristen fished out a treat from her pocket and gave it to Seagn. The dog watched attentively. Seagn tossed it to the dog, who caught it on the fly.

"Thanks for letting me know." Kristen got up and hugged Seagn. "Good luck and be careful."

Seagn returned the hug. "I will. And thanks."

Seagn had tears in her eyes as she left the shelter probably for the last time for many months.

•　　•　　•

Seagn opened the door to The Hexx Shop — one of the many metaphysical stores located in the mecca of Salem. *One last person to tell and then I can go pack.*

"Hey, Shaun," called the Rubenesque woman behind the counter. She wore a black dress — the typical color of "witches of Salem". She even owned a pointed witch's hat that she wore on occasion. But this time around, it was quiet in the town and she didn't wear the full accoutrements of what was expected of a witch in Salem.

"Hiya, Anna."

"Cup of tea?"

"No, I'm not staying long. I'm going away for a little while."

"Oh? Bahamas?"

"Heh, I wish. No, I'm running away to join the circus."

Anna clapped her hands and smiled broadly. "Oh, that calls for a reading!"

"No, really, Anna —"

But she had already ducked a hand under the counter and came up with a velvet bag. "Just three cards."

Seagn sighed and rolled her eyes. "All right."

Anna shuffled the cards, humming to herself. "Okay, shuffle."

Seagn shuffled the larger than usual tarot cards. Awkward in her hands, she made a mess of the shuffle and had to gather them up one by one.

Anna took the deck and fanned out the cards. "Pick three."

Seagn chose one near the bottom, one in the middle, and the top card, handing them to Anna who turned them over and gazed at the pictures.

The first colorful card showed an enraptured couple standing together with their arms entwined around a pair of cups. An angel with spread wings over them to bless them.

Next to that was a card that read, "The Devil" on the bottom, a man with horns sitting on a black block, and two people chained to him.

The last card showed a young boy working on a wood carving.

"You're going to find love," said Anna, pointing to the first card. "Or at least lust." She tapped the second card, The Devil. "You'll work hard, but you'll enjoy it." She picked up the card with boy carving five-pointed stars in wood and showed it to her

"That's it?"

"That's only three cards. If you want a full reading, you'll have to pay for it."

"You know how I feel about this," Seagn said with a small chuckle. "But I'll take your advice under consideration."

"Are you moving out, then?" Anna gathered the cards up.

"No. I'll still send you an automatic check every month. It might be until just the winter, I don't know."

"You don't know?"

"I'll be saving animals."

Anna frowned. "If that's what you need to do."

"Hey, I'll find love there. You said so."

"That Devil card worries me."

Seagn smiled. "I don't believe in it, so it can't hurt me, right?"

"Spirit does what it's meant to do: influence our lives."

Seagn waved a hand, which they both knew was a dismissive gesture. "Shifting subjects without a clutch: if someone needs to couch surf you can rent the room out. I don't have anything of value there." Items of value were in a storage unit in Boston, where she and Liam, her brother, had a key and could take things out as needed.

"It's your sacred space," said Anna.

Seagn tried hard not to roll her eyes again. *These metaphysical types*, she thought as she headed toward the door.

"Well, good luck."

Seagn put her hand on the doorhandle said over her shoulder, "Oh, hey, about Lemonade." Seagn threaded off the VW's key from her ring. "Take her out for a spin once a week or so."

Anna caught the key Seagn tossed her. "Will do."

Seagn waved and went back outside, to the door next to the shop. It led up a set of stairs to her two-room apartment — well, three rooms if you wanted to include the bathroom.

She gathered her suitcase to pack a week's worth of clothes into it. She also dug out her emergency vet's kit, with medicine and vials. She didn't know if that would be enough for her use, or even if they were applicable, considering there were about twenty farm animals.

Twenty lethargic and sick animals.

She left the apartment, passing by her VW. She patted the car's hood. "I'll be back. Be good for Anna."

Then she walked the mile and a half back to the carnival grounds.

2

S EAGN PULLED OUT THE CASHIER'S CHECK from her pocket and placed it on the table. Webby's piggy eyes went wide, seeing the amount.

"Where's the contract?"

"You're an independent contractor," said Webby. The woman, who Seagn guessed by now was his wife, showed up holding a clipboard and a fiftieth-generation copy of some blurred words with a clear signature line at the bottom. "You pay your own way to and from the gigs. You've got a truck and a trailer and the animals and tents. You have to hire your own crew to set up and tear down unless you can do it yourself."

"Understood," she said. "What's this contract say? I can't read hardly any of it."

"Says what I just told you."

"I don't see the word 'trailer' in this."

Said the wife, "It's a boilerplate for independent contractors."

"So, I pay my own taxes, my own upkeep, my own gas, my own feed —"

"And we let you squat at our gigs," said Webby. "You get a percent of the take."

Seagn tried to study the mangled contract. "One percent? That's bullshit."

The wife took the contract and scratched out the word "one" and added "3%". "That's what Fatsy got."

In the first month, Seagn already knew she was going to have to pay out to get those animals up to snuff. That was why she took out a total of ten thousand dollars to start. She had about twenty grand left over from the sale of her parents' house, along with a Primus ATM card so could get her money at any time from any bank or store.

"Three percent of what?"

Webby said, with a sigh, "What we make."

"Which could be …?"

"Three hundred dollars a day," said the wife, giving Webby an angry look. "On average."

"Where do you usually go?"

"Southern New England and lower New York."

Webby kept his eyes on the check. The wife kept eye contact with Seagn.

"What about the winter?"

"That's up to you," said Webby. "Slaughter 'em for all —"

Both Seagn and the wife glared at Webby.

"We can come to an arrangement when the time comes," said the wife.

"Look," said Webby, as he reached for the check, "we can talk about all this stuff as it comes up."

Seagn put her hand on the check. "Where's Fatsy?"

"Drinking his severance." The wife snorted in response.

Seagn removed her hand, and Webby snatched up the check. "Congratulations, you own some farm animals."

"A petting zoo," said Seagn, rising from the chair. "I keep what I make from them."

"How can you make money with a petting zoo?"

Seagn smiled. "You agree I keep the money I make from them."

His wife sat back, crossing her arms. Webby passed the check through his fingers.

"We'll see."

"Draw up an agreement." Seagn picked up a pen. "Not this thing. And I want a copy."

"Yeah, you'll get one." Webby signed under her name, and the wife snatched up the paper. She went into the RV.

"Beer?" Webby asked, turning to a cooler under the RV.

"No thanks."

"Tear down is at nine. You gotta make the place look like nothin's been there."

Seagn nodded.

Then the woman stepped out of the RV, handing a piece of paper to Seagn. It was a badly-rendered copy of the paper she had signed.

"You need a new scanner," Seagn said.

"It works," said the wife.

Webby grinned at Seagn. "It's all yours now, honey.".

She glanced in the direction of the animals' tent and stifled a sigh. *Yeah. All mine.*

•   •   •

Seagn approached the animals from the northern side of the carnival. All of them were enclosed in segregated fenced pens.

She approached the cow first. Her pen was barely big enough for her to lay down. She ambled to the entrance of the pen and gazed at Seagn.

"I'll take care of you," she told them. "All of you."

Next, she examined at then animals in the pen next to the cow. Five goats gathered at the doorway. One goat lay on the opposite side of the door to the pen, uninterested in what the other goats were doing.

After the goats stood a miniature pony, tied to a large temporary aluminum fence, nowhere near the water. He didn't even look at her. She immediately untied the pony and opened the gate leading him to the water trough.

Opposite the pony, three sheep, a ram, and two pigs shared the same pen. Nowhere was there any hay for comfort, or barely enough space for the animals to stretch out. One water trough was at the center, a long walk for the cow if she could get out of the pen. There was no food anywhere that she could see.

She unlatched the pen to the first set of goats and stepped inside, closing the latch behind her. Finally, the goat at the end of the pen raised its head. The other goats romped around Seagn, pulling on her shirt, making noises that sounded to her like "*Please, please, …*"

Seagn went over to the goat lying in his own filth. He bleated sorrowfully, and it shattered Seagn's heart.

Ignoring the dirt, crap, and mud, she bent and picked up the goat. He only made a small noise, but didn't fight her. She carried him to the pen's entrance, unlatching the door again. The other goats gathered among themselves in the middle of the pen, as if afraid to leave.

The goat weighed light in her arms, not any heavier than a large golden retriever. She continued to the semi's trailer, which was locked tight.

She put the goat down and it collapsed in a heap at the back entrance of the trailer. It was starting to get dark, and she didn't have any light to clearly see the goat or the lock. Around her, the carnival came to life, lights and noise filling the air.

Seagn gathered the goat and put him in the pen next to the trailer with the pigs and sheep. She went around to the front of the trailer, where a large Peterbilt truck sat parked. It looked old and just as worn out as the animals. She tried the driver's side door; it swung open on creaky hinges.

The overhead light came on while she climbed into the cab. She wrinkled her nose at the stench of sweat and bad B.O. Animal crap she could deal with. But this, not so much.

She pushed back curtains that separated the driver and passenger from the back of the cab. The stink was worse back here.

An unmade cot sat in the wan light of the cab, clothes piled upon it. It sagged in the middle. Centerfold pictures of naked women surrounded the walls around the cot. Seagn leaned back from the stench and from the thoughts that went through her head as to why there were naked girls plastered on the wall.

Eight thousand dollars said that this was hers now.

She opened the passenger door to air out the cab and dove back into the area with the cot. She stripped the cot, bundling the clothes and the pictures into a neat pile, then tied the ends of the sheet together. She tossed the bundle out of the truck.

That got rid of some of the stink. She saw other things under the cot, and dug them out. They smelled horrible: clothes containing unwashed underwear and left-over condoms. She put a hand to her stomach to stop herself from retching. However, those ended up out on the grass, too.

She climbed down from the truck and noticed someone walking along the animals in the dark. She looked around for a weapon. Instead, she hit the side of the trailer, sending a booming metallic sound into the night.

"Hello?" called a man's voice.

"Who's there?" Seagn demanded.

"Moose."

She furrowed her brow in confusion and headed toward the animals. A tall man stood silhouetted against the bright lights of the carnival. He held up something that jingled. "Webby said you might need these."

Seagn approached the man. The man could see her clearly with the back light, but she couldn't see him. He handed keys to her.

"Thanks. Moose?"

The man nodded and said, "That's what they call me here, anyways."

"You wouldn't happen to have a flashlight?"

He patted down his pockets, pulling out a plastic lighter. He flicked the switch, and his face was illuminated. He had a mustache, something she didn't expect, and shoulder-length mouse-brown hair. His eyes were dark in the dim light.

"This okay?"

"Yes, thank you."

She went to the trailer and unlocked the door. Again, on squeaky hinges, she pulled open the trailer door and got a whiff of crap, urine, and old hay.

"Oh, my God, really?" She peered in the dark recesses of the trailer that the light didn't even penetrate.

"Whatsematter?"

"When was the last time this got mucked out?"

He let go of the plastic piece that kept the lighter on and plunged them into relative darkness. "Ain' never seen it clean."

She looked toward the animals. "No wonder. Jesus."

"Yeah," said Moose. "Fatsy never took care of 'em."

"Why didn't anyone say anything?"

"He an' Webby are like this." He crossed his fingers.

"It didn't sound like it," Seagn muttered. "Thanks for the keys."

"Don't mention it. I'll be seein' you at tear down. I drive the truck. What's your name, anyways?"

"Shaun."

"Nice name." He probably smiled at her, but she couldn't see it. "See ya 'round."

As he turned to leave, she said, "Wait."

"Hm?"

"Can you drive the truck for me tomorrow?"

"Well, yeah, we tear down tomorrow."

"I mean in the morning. I want to get this trailer cleaned up."

"You're gonna have to take it to a car wash."

"Probably. Though I have some favors I can call in."

Then she heard Webby's voice, "Hey, what the fuck!"

"Gotta go," said Moose, as he ran off. Seagn opened her mouth to say, "bye", but he was long gone.

Webby's large frame filled the north entrance of the tent. "What the fuck you doin'? We're on."

"These animals are in no condition to be displayed."

"Then you get jack shit for today."

Seagn shrugged. "Or tomorrow. I need to check them over to see if they're sick or injured. One of the goats needs tending to."

"Who the fuck cares?"

"You will if they get some kid sick with a bovine flu and they trace it back to you."

Webby seemed to chew the inside of his cheek. "Put on the lights."

"Any idea how?"

"Search me." Webby waved a hand and walked away.

Muttering "Asshole" under her breath, Seagn went back to the tent. She could barely see the lights strung up under the tent and tried to follow the wires. They were a hopeless tangle in the middle. One wire led to the back of the trailer. That wire flowed down the inside of the door, to a large black blob against the wall.

Invest in flashlights, she thought, as she felt around the black blob. It was square in shape, with grooves at one side. Her hand brushed against something. Suddenly, a loud bang burst in front of her.

Seagn jumped back as she saw the lights flicker on around the farm animals. Many of them made noises, bleating and *baa*-ing. They rushed to the gates. They must have been conditioned that lights on meant showtime.

Lights inside of the trailer also came on. Now she could see deeper within it.

And it was a mess. Old wet hay, crap, with plenty of room for laying down in this trailer. Some of the pens were separated from others by the same temporary fencing that was outside. Obviously Fatsy thought this was comfort.

Seagn climbed up and walked into the trailer, which was as long as a semi's trailer, and covered by a worn tarp on top. Rusted gratings surrounded her instead of solid aluminum walls of a tractor-trailer, giving air and light to the animals when they were in the trailer. There was plenty of room, which said to her that there had originally been more animals than there now were outside.

Seagn jumped down to see that people were walking by her display of the animals, not stopping, heading directly into the carnival. She knew they were all was a sorry sight. But she had plans and ideas to make these animals be the highlight of the show.

•   •   •

The carnival lasted until about ten. During that time, Seagn cleaned out the pens the animals were locked in; she rearranged the fencing so they had room to lay down.

She carried the sick goat — that she named Tommy — into the trailer and examined him under the brighter lights inside.

He bleated as she touched a spot near his stomach, noting that the skin there felt hot and inflamed. An infection, or an ulcer of some sort. No wonder he wasn't eating. She turned to her emergency vet bag. She didn't have his exact weight but guessed at it from carrying him. She eyeballed a syringe full of antibiotics.

She gave him the shot and realized that she would have to get more antibiotics and other items. *I shouldn't have quit the practice like I did*, she thought. Now she'd have to somehow get prescription medicines by mail order. She knew she couldn't give the pharmaceutical companies the PO box where she normally got her mail; she would have to give them a physical address. Unless she could purchase them from the clinic ...

That meant she'd have to come back to Salem every week or so to get her stock refilled. She could also look for vets in the towns they were going to and probably purchase their stock. She needed to talk to Webby to find out what towns they were heading to, so she could pre-order medicines to arrive when she got there.

In the trailer, she found a bag of feed intended for horses, not for cows, sheep, or goats. Also, she found the remains of a dead cat. She closed her eyes for a moment, tamping down the anger — and the bile — that threatened to come up. She dug out a rusty old shovel, scooped the lifeless cat up and, after saying a little prayer that she always muttered whenever putting an animal to sleep, she placed the cat into a bag and carried it to a dumpster.

"Sorry," she muttered, dropping the dead cat into the dumpster. She hated getting rid of animals like that, wanting instead to cremate them and deliver the ashes to someone who had loved that poor creature.

Seagn soon realized why the cat was needed, as she found signs of mice living among the hay. She knew of a couple of mousers living in the shelter that she could adopt and use in the trailer. She fed the animals with the inappropriate bag of feed, hoping they wouldn't get sick.

At ten on the button, the lights and music died at the carnival. People streamed out past her display, glancing at the animals who stared out at them. The goats bleated and the cow snorted. No one stopped.

It wasn't like the display was inviting. She'd have to invest in some interesting fencing and bunting to spruce up the display. A trip to Michael's or Hobby Lobby was in order. Seagn took out a notebook from her emergency kit and started making a list of things to buy.

"Shut the fuckin' lights off," yelled someone from the carnival area.

Seagn almost yelled, "Fuck you," back, but kept her composure. She went to the generator, saw the switch, and switched it off.

The area darkened, but her eyes adjusted to the dim light of the gibbous moon. The animals still gathered at the entrance to the gates, waiting.

Seagn was not about to let the animals in the dirty mess that was the trailer; not until after she cleaned it up in the morning. They would have to spend the night outside under the tent.

Which meant she had to stay up to watch them.

With no caffeine.

Seagn listened to the animals settle down. She walked up and down the aisle as the animals fell asleep. The cow, that she had named Bella, was the first to snore.

She jumped up to sit on the edge of the trailer, her feet dangling off it.

"Shaun?" called Moose in the dark. He held a flashlight pointed at the ground, as he picked his way among the pens.

"Over here," responded Seagn as the flashlight jerked up, aiming in her direction, illuminating her feet.

"I got you a flashlight," he said, walking over to her. He offered her another flashlight that was off. "They had 'em at the hardware store nearby."

"I appreciate it, thank you. What do I owe you?"

"Pshaw, nothin."

Seagn smiled, tested the flashlight out by aiming it at him. He was tall, broad-shouldered, and handsome in a rough sort of way. He winced when she shined the light toward his face. "Hey, that's a 56 Mag light."

"Sorry," she said with a chuckle. "I just wanted to see you clearly."

"You can see me tomorrow morning. Speaking of which, what time?"

The shelter opened at ten, but she knew sometimes people were there early. If she provided donuts and coffee, maybe they'd let her use the hose and a volunteer.

"Nine?"

"I'll be up at sunrise for Sunday breakfast. That'll give me plenty of time." He sat down on the trailer. His legs didn't dangle like hers did. "You paying me for this, right?"

"Uh …"

He snorted.

"Yes," Seagn said quickly. "How much?"

"Same as Webby. Ten an hour."

"Cash, I suppose."

"If you don't mind."

She calculated. "How about thirty dollars for four hours?"

"Thirty-five."

"Fine."

He held out his hand. She shook it, trying to be firm and not dainty. He closed his strong hand around hers and pumped it once before letting go. She could tell that he had restrained himself.

"So, what made you buy the animals here, Shaun?"

"They're in deplorable condition. I can make them better."

"At least you care."

"Don't you?"

"None of my business," he said. He patted his breast pocket. "Wanna smoke?"

"No, I don't smoke, but thanks." She turned the darkened flashlight over in her hands. "Webby's the head honcho here?"

"Sure." He threaded out a cigarette from his breast pocket and a lighter from his jeans. "Steph's second."

"His wife?"

"Yep. She ain't too bad. Webby treats most of us like we're dumb as rocks." He lit the cigarette and took in a deep drag. "Not to say that some of the people he hires ain't dumb as rocks. You don't seem to be."

Seagn laughed. "I hope not."

"He'll talk to you like you're fuckin' stupid. S'cuse my French."

"I've noticed. And don't worry. I have a feeling I'll be hearing the f-bomb an awful lot around here."

He chuckled, blew out smoke. "Yeah, an awful lot."

Then she heard someone at the truck yelling, "What the fuck?"

"Fatsy," said Moose.

"What the fuck is my shit doin' out here?"

"Keep it down," Moose called. "Curfew."

"I'll fuckin' tell you when it's curfew, you mother fucking wetback."

Seagn winced, but Moose just let out another burst of smoke. Seagn heard Fatsy waddle to her end of the trailer. "You fuckin' bitch."

"I own this trailer, these animals, and that truck as of two p.m. today."

"Yesterday," said Moose through the smoke coming out of his nose. "It's almost midnight."

"I don't give a flying rat's ass what the fuck time — you got no right —"

"Uh, excuse me?" Seagn did not jump down from the trailer, because if she did, she'd have to look up at Fatsy. Instead, she stood up so Fatsy would have to look up at her. "I told you to get your stuff out. It's not my fault you spent the time at a bar."

"You fuckin' bitch," he repeated.

"Gather your stuff and get out. You're lucky I didn't toss it in the dumpster with the dead cat."

Moose turned his head toward her. "You found a dead cat?"

"In the trailer." She bent down to Fatsy's eye level. "You know, I could report you to the authorities for abusing animals."

Fatsy crossed his arms. "I don't do nuthin'. I feed 'em an' shit."

"Horse kibble and water?"

"They're alive, ain't they?"

"How many farm animals did you have when you started?"

He didn't look at her when he answered, his eyes focused on a spot above her head. "Twenty or so. I dunno."

Seagn moved to try to catch his eye, but he only shrugged and turned away.

"They're yours now," he said over his shoulder, as he went to his bundle and picked it up from the grass. "Have fun with it."

"Asshole," Seagn muttered, sitting back down. Moose snuffed out his cigarette, dropping the butt on the ground and stomping on it just to make sure it was out.

"Yep, he is. He's probably going to be our supe now."

"Supervisor?"

Moose nodded. "Like I said, him and Webby." He glanced toward the animals. "What're you gonna do tonight?"

"What do you mean?"

"You gonna leave them here? Somebody can come and bust them out."

"I have to stay up and watch them."

Moose said, "Lemme get a few z's and I'll come over around two and take over for you."

"Are you sure?"

"Sure. I can take a nap in the truck later."

"Thanks. I really appreciate it."

Moose jumped down off the trailer. "You owe me a pack of cigs."

"Done."

He flicked on the flashlight and started back to the carnival. Seagn watched the bobbing light until it disappeared.

3

S EAGN FELT SOMEONE SHAKE HER just moments after she fell asleep. "Sunrise," said a man's gentle voice.

She pulled the threadbare blanket over her head and moaned. The animals were already up and looking to her for food. All she had was the bag of horse kibble.

Sunrise illuminated the animals a lot more clearly. The sheep were matted; the goats, though they pranced, did so in the mess of hay, crap, and urine; Bella didn't look like she moved from her spot in the pen. The horse whinnied loudly.

"God," she whispered, looking at the animals. "This is worse than I thought."

Moose touched her arm. "I got you a coffee."

She shook her head. "I don't drink coffee."

"How do you function?" He held two cups from Dunkin' in his hands.

"Tea. I drink tea. I have to feed them. Then we can go to the animal shelter."

"Why there?"

"That's where I'm going to clean out the trailer."

"Oh," Moose said. "Who's going to watch the animals?"

She hadn't thought of that.

"Let me see if anyone's up. You're going to have to pay them."

"The usual rate?"

"At least."

Seagn gathered the food and put it in some troughs, bringing them to the animals. They were excited for the food, and she knew that her petting zoo idea would work well for them. Moose returned with a half-awake skinny kid who wore glasses and looked like he slept in his clothes.

"This is Beau."

"Hallo," he said, his French accent coming through with just that one word.

"Morning," Seagn said, holding out her hand. The second cup of Moose's coffee was in the young man's other hand. "Can you watch the animals for a few hours?"

"How much?"

"Fifty."

"*Merde*, yeah."

Moose narrowed his eyes.

"It's an emergency," said Seagn, walking back to the trailer. She acted like she was getting money from the inside of the truck, when she actually had it on her person.

"Come back at eight," she said, handing Beau two twenties and two fives.

"Uh," said Moose, "Pay him after."

Beau gave Moose a glare. "I'm good for it," he snapped, taking the money.

"Better be." Beau shrugged off Moose's angry look and headed back to the carnival.

"First rule," said Moose to Seagn. "Pay after the job is done."

"That include you?"

"I wouldn't be offended if you did."

"I was going to give you forty."

"If it's four hours, yeah. More'n that, you have to cough it up."

She took out a ten from her pocket. "Can you get me a cup of tea with cream and two sugars and a bacon, egg, and cheese sandwich?"

"Sure," he said, taking the money.

"Keep the change."

He laughed, and headed past her display, down the street to the small Dunkin' that was just past the Commons. The animals were satisfied with their food, although she wasn't.

She disconnected the wire that led from the tent to the generator. There were three gas cans next to the generator. One sloshed with fluid; the other two were empty. She took out her notebook and added "gas for generator" on her list.

Moose returned with her tea and two white bags. He handed one to her. "Bought me some donuts."

She opened her bag and smelled bacon. "Donuts are bad for you."

"Yeah, so's smoking. What of it?"

Seagn took out the bagel sandwich and leaned against the trailer, eating it. "So, what brings you to the carnival, Moose?"

He shrugged, eating a jelly donut stick. "The only place that hires anybody."

"You're not just anybody," she said.

"Never graduated high school. You can't even get a job at McDonald's without a high school diploma." He bit into the jelly stick and spoke with his mouth full. "Ran away to join the carnival at 17."

She chewed and swallowed. "You've been here since you were 17?"

"On and off," he said. "Tried to get a real job a few times. I didn't like being stuck in a building for more than eight hours."

He turned to her. "So, what about you? You wanted to save these animals. How come?"

"I'm a vet. It's my calling, I guess you could say."

"Ohhhh. That means you're a lot smarter than Webby."

She grinned. "We'll have to see about that."

After the donut, Moose had a smoke, while Seagn walked around and made sure the latches on the enclosures were in place. Beau arrived at eight on the dot, carrying a folding chair with him.

"Might as well get comfortable, no?"

"Might as well." She called to Moose, "Okay, whenever you're ready."

Moose went to the driver's side and started up the truck. It came to life immediately. Seagn locked up the trailer, made sure nothing was tied to it (like the tent) and climbed into the passenger's side. She gave him directions to the shelter.

Moose handled the truck deftly through the narrow streets of Salem, the large red semi slowly picking its way along, making sure to take wide turns.

They arrived at the shelter in half an hour. Two cars were parked out front, and Seagn saw the Animal Control Officer's SUV parked in the back. Kristen was always early to help feed the dogs.

"Where do you want me to park?"

"Can you back up to where the SUV is? The hoses lead from there."

He parked the trailer about three feet away from the ACO's SUV. Seagn climbed out as she saw Kristen come out to see what was going on.

"Oh, hey," said Kristen upon seeing Seagn. "What's this?"

"My new project from the carnival. Kristen, meet Moose."

Kristen nodded to him and turned to Seagn. "What brings you here?"

"I need to use the hoses. This trailer is disgusting."

Kristen looked at the trailer. "Awful big trailer."

"It's going to take us a couple of hours or more."

"Let me see if Mike is available."

Mike was one of the volunteers. Trish's adopted son, he had Down's but a sweet disposition, and did anything you asked.

"He can use the hose," called Seagn as Kristen walked back into the shelter. "He'd like that."

Moose patted his breast pocket. "Gonna have to get more smokes."

"We'll stop somewhere on the way."

Seagn walked over to the back of the trailer, unlocked it, and swung the doors wide open. The stench wasn't as bad as it hit her yesterday; she was probably nose-blind now.

Mike, grinning and excited, came out with a long fire hose. "Hey, Doc! I'm here for the cleaning!"

"Great, Mike. You'll have to start in the back. Oh, and get the rubber boots."

Mike looked down at his Converses. "Right!" he dropped the fire hose and ran back into the shelter. Kristen came out and shook her head.

"I need to also adopt a mouser," Seagn said to Kristen.

"You have a pest problem?"

"They'll probably hide when Mike hoses them out."

"Chief might be good. And Maisey."

Maisey always brought presents. Chief lounged about most of the time, but he had been the mouser in the shelter before Maisey.

"I'll take Maisey. Give Chief back his old job."

"Sounds good. You have to fill out the paperwork."

Mike came back out, clunking in his big rubber boots. "I'm ready now!"

"Moose —"

"On it. C'mere." Moose jumped into the trailer and helped Mike onto it.

"Whew, it stinks!" Mike said, waving his hand in front of his face.

"That's why we have to clean it," Seagn said.

Moose walked into the depths of the trailer. She heard the water go on, and a whoop from Mike as he started hosing it down.

Seagn followed Kristen into the shelter and stopped by Maisey's cage. Maisey knew her and rubbed up against her hand when she thrust it into the cage. "Hey, sweetie." Seagn got purrs in response.

Seagn paid the adoption fee, filled out the paperwork, and got Maisey in a temporary carrier. Maisey meowed pitifully, confused as to what was going on. They went outside to see that half of the trailer was sparkling clean, and a medium sized pile of hay and crap lay outside between the trailer and the SUV.

"Want me to call Wright's?" asked Kristen. "They probably have plenty of hay you can buy."

Wright's Chicken and Dairy Farm was north of Salem in Lynn, out of Kristen's jurisdiction, but familiar to the Boston area.

"Yeah, could you?"

Kristen had her phone in her hand and started to dial.

Seagn went to the trailer to see how it was going. Mike waved the hose haphazardly, screaming in delight, while Moose would help aim it at the correct angle. Both of them were soaked with water. Moose's white shirt was plastered to his broad chest, and his long hair dripped. He shivered at the cold water.

She put Maisey in the truck's passenger side. A burst of water sprayed through the grates and barely missed her. She decided to stay out of range and go back into the shelter.

The pile of hay got larger and more smelly.

About an hour later, Moose and Mike had finished the cleaning. Dripping wet, they jumped down from the trailer.

Kristen returned with towels. "Wright's said they're open for you."

Moose dried off his hair first.

"That was fun!" Mike said, rubbing his wet shirt with the towel. "What next?"

Moose waved the towel at the pile of hay. "We get rid of that."

"Okay!" Mike raised the hose.

"No," said Moose, grabbing the hose from him. "Shovels and trash bags."

"Compost," said Kristen. "We can put it in the lawn bags and I'll bring them to the town compost pile."

Moose shrugged. "Whatever."

Moose rolled up the heavy hose. Kristen found shovels and paper bags, and all four of them tackled the hay pile.

Another half hour, and they had finished that.

"The trip back will dry off the trailer," said Seagn, as she jumped into the trailer. Now looking and smelling better, she examined the pens a little more closely.

There were eighteen pens, nine on each side with an aisle in the middle, none with locks, all with latches. Most of the latches worked, while others were too rusty to move. There was plenty of space for the number of animals she had. She didn't know if there were any more mice in the trailer, but Maisey was going to make sure none remained.

"Okay, next is the farm, then feed."

"You should look into getting a car or something," said Moose, after getting into the truck. "Other than bringing this all over the place."

She pondered that. The VW wouldn't fit in the trailer. A bicycle was too slow. A moped? They weren't very safe. She knew of too many accidents on mopeds.

•　　•　　•

Seagn stopped at the ATM and took out another two hundred dollars after leaving most of her cash at Wright's farm. They were kind enough to sell her the feed she needed for Bella, since they had plenty. They also told her where to get feed for the other animals. It was in the middle of Lynn, narrow streets and tight corners, but Moose got through it.

They pulled into the carnival ten minutes before it opened. Beau got up and ran off, leaving his chair behind him, as soon as the truck turned the corner.

The trailer pulled in, smelling of sweet hay and loaded with proper food. Seagn had also bought some extra troughs, hoses, and other implements of farming life, such as shovels, rakes, and a pitchfork.

Moose parked the trailer and jumped out of the cab. "Gotta go."

He took off into the carnival. She hadn't paid him, but she knew he'd be back. She *hoped* he'd be back.

Seagn examined the animals while the carnival went on. Most of them were healthy, which said a lot about their constitution. She began naming them.

The sick goat she had already named Tommy, then there was Bella. For ease of remembering, she named the pony Shet, short for Shetland. She examined his hooves and saw he needed new horseshoes, since two out of the four were broken. The two pigs were named Sable for the black one, and Tiny, for the mottled one, even though they both were pretty big.

She couldn't tell the difference between the sheep, but she named them Huey, Dewey, and Louie. The ram got named Bob.

She named the remaining five goats: Jack for the one with half a horn; Jill for the pretty mottled girl; Alise for the white one — well, off-white because she was dirty; Mako for a brown, black, and gold old goat; and Mohawk, who had a black Mohawk-looking stripe on the top of his otherwise white head.

Tommy, the sick goat, stayed in his area in the back of the pen, lying down and bleating helplessly. Seagn carried him to the trailer, and also let Maisey loose in the hay. She was confused at first, frightened, and ran off into a corner. Seagn set down some cat food for her and locked the doors.

She left the animals and headed to Webby's trailer. Webby wasn't there, but Stephanie was inside the RV. It was chilly and overcast on this early April Sunday afternoon, so there weren't a lot of people at the carnival.

"Hey, do you have a list of where we're going?"

"We'll be in Worcester next weekend," Steph called from inside the trailer.

"Worcester is a big city."

"At the opening of a Costco."

"So, you don't have a list."

She finally came to the door. She wore a sweatshirt, a hoodie, and jeans. Seagn could hear an inkjet printer in the background.

"This isn't final," said Stephanie. "Things change all the time."

She retreated into the trailer and returned with a piece of paper. Dates and places for April, two for May, a smattering for June, July, August, nothing for September, one for October were hand-written on what looked like a notebook sheet of paper.

"Some of these have two on the same weekend."

"Yeah, we split up. You go where there's room."

"Is there room in Worcester?"

"Hell if I know," Stephanie snapped. "Go check the address out and see."

If it was the opening of a Costco, it was probably a parking lot. How would she set up the tent on asphalt?

"I'm going to need help taking down the display today."

"Yeah? Hire a day laborer."

"I was wondering if I could hire Moose."

"He can go work for you when he's not working for us. He's *our* independent contractor, just like everyone here. And what was Beau doing?"

"Watching the animals. I don't want to leave them alone."

Stephanie snorted, went back into the trailer, slamming shut the screen door behind her.

What the hell did that mean?

•   •   •

The overcast chilly day continued, with a slow trickle of people going to the brightly-lit carnival. A couple of people gazed over the sad display of animals but walked on.

Prepared at dusk with a flashlight, Seagn put on the generator. The animals got excited again when the lights burst on.

"Maybe I'm supposed to feed them again," she muttered to no one in particular. She should have asked Fatsy. Or Webby. Nah, she doubted he knew or cared anything about the animals other than making sure they were at the gigs.

She assumed that her purpose was to display farm animals to city people as a circus side show. Seagn wanted people to touch the animals, to run their hand through (cleaner) wool, to feed them a handful at a time, to ride the pony, to feel the cow's ragged tongue lick their hand.

She opened the door and Maisey came to her, presenting her with a dead mouse about the size of the cat's head. She smelled of hay and farm as Seagn patted her.

"Good girl," she said, and took the mouse by the tail, tossing it in a plastic bag.

When she put the lid back down on the dumpster, large drops of water hit her hand. She looked up as a drop hit her lip.

"Shit," she whispered, walking back to the animals. The tent protected them from the rain, and the tarp covering the trailer would protect them inside — mostly. That morning she had seen threadbare areas of the tarp and sections where the ropes caused holes to split at the top.

Seagn chased Maisey to a pen near the front of the trailer and closed it behind her. She was a cat; she could jump over the fencing if she wanted, but Seagn hoped that Maisey would stay put.

The rain came down steadily, drumming against the tent. She watched people leave the carnival, heads bent against the cold rain. Some rain blew into the tent. Seagn shook her head against it, and the animals gathered in bunches for warmth.

Screw this.

She connected the ramp she had found to the trailer, then walked down the aisle and went to see Bella, who had it the worst, since she was at the entrance to the tent.

Seagn unlocked the latch and guided Bella toward the trailer. Bella walked unsteadily at first, since she had been locked in a pen standing up without any room; but eventually got her legs under her. She walked up the ramp without any problem.

When Bella got into the aisle of the trailer, she kept walking. Seagn held onto her bridle, but Bella walked to the very front of the trailer. She turned left and went into a wide pen, sniffing the hay. She walked around in a circle, then lay down, her back to the grate where the rain came through.

"Okay, so this is your spot. Good to know."

Next, Seagn got the pigs. They were too big to carry, so she had to guide them with a broom. Sable and Tiny squealed when she locked them in a pen. She returned to them with a trough she bought.

The rain darkened the sky even more. It was a cold, miserable early April shower, with remnants of the winter hidden in its drops and wind.

Seagn worked on getting the sheep into the trailer when she heard Fatsy scream from a distance, "What the fuck you doin'?"

Seagn jerked to a stop, but the sheep kept walking, going up the ramp into the trailer.

"It's raining."

"It's not fuckin' nine yet!" Fatsy got closer. "You got more'n three fuckin' hours."

"But it's raining."

"So?"

"Do you see anyone at the carnival?"

"That don't matter."

The sheep disappeared into the trailer. The goats gathered near the entrance to their pen, bleating to get out.

"No one's coming," Seagn said, turning from Fatsy back to the trailer.

"Oh, yeah?" called Fatsy. "You watch."

Seagn saw the sheep had already gathered in a pen.

Well, she thought, *at least the animals were trained to get back into the trailer.*

She went out to get the horse and saw Webby barreling out of the carnival in her direction. He yelled at her, "It's not closing time yet!"

"Nobody's going to come."

Webby ducked under the tent, his face red and he breathed heavily. "You have to stay open until nine. Didn't Fatsy just tell you?"

"He came over screaming at me," Seagn said. "It's raining."

"It's raining now, but that could change! Put those animals back out right now. Or I won't pay you for the day." He turned around among the empty pens. "God damn pieces of shit. Never should have bought them."

Seagn stood holding the horse's bridle. The goats gathered at the entrance to their pen, thinking they were going to get out.

"Fine," Seagn said, letting go of the bridle and shouldering the horse back into his pen.

Bella looked comfortable lying in the hay, so she didn't bother to get her out. The pigs didn't want to come back out, so she had to herd them out to the pens. The sheep also gave her a hard time.

By the time she had the set-up again, the rain came down in sheets, blowing into the tent, and making her and the animals miserable. They shivered in the cold rain while she stewed about Webby barking orders at her.

"I left the practice because of a bitch," she told the goats. "Now it's the same thing — except the guy's an asshole."

At nine sharp, it was still raining, but the lights went out in the carnival, except for a few spotlights that came on. No spotlights came on in her direction, so she had to work by the generator lights and flashlight.

She muttered darkly as she got the animals settled in the trailer, then took apart the fencing. Each piece was so heavy she could carry only one at a time. After putting away only one fence, the generator died.

"Shit."

She dropped the fencing on her foot and bit back another curse. She got out her flashlight from next to the generator, found the full gas can, and tried to figure out where to pour the gas.

It took her a while, but she found two places to pour liquid into. One had a little oil can on the lid, so she knew it wasn't that one. She poured the gas into the second available hole. The generator sputtered.

She shut it off, continued pouring the gasoline in. When she finished, she closed the lid, turned it on. Again, it sputtered for a moment, then started.

Seagn started gathering the fencing again, then looked at the tent and how it was set up. She untied its moorings, pulling up stakes. Next, she pulled in the lights.

The carnival was taken apart already. Lights came down as she watched.

She unplugged the lights and wrapped them around a fence for ease of taking them out again. Seagn then sat down on the edge of the trailer, just to take a rest.

The next thing she knew, she pitched forward, falling off the trailer, face-first onto the grass.

That woke her up. Luckily, she wasn't injured, just surprised.

"I see you're not done yet," said Moose, watching her get up from the fall.

Her face burned. "I, uh …"

He waved his hand. "Happens to everyone the first few times. Once you sit down, that's when it hits you. Lemme help you with the tent."

Moose started pulling the poles up. She followed suit, diagonally across from him. He undid the poles' tops from the tent's rings, and let the tent fall to the ground.

"You can't fold the tent when it's wet like this," he said. "It'll get all moldy."

"What do I do?"

"Take one end." He took the other, and they manhandled the tent into the trailer. He used the rings and some rope to tie the tent's edges to the fencing inside the trailer. However, the middle of the tent sagged with a puddle in the middle.

Moose looked up at the tarp roof, but there was nothing he could tie the tent's center to. "The minute we get somewhere that's dry, we gotta take the tent out."

She nodded. Moose shut off the generator, closed the back of the trailer, and locked it. "Now we go park at The Ranch."

"A real ranch?"

He laughed as he walked to the front of the truck. "Nah."

Seagn saw him pick up a duffel bag that he had left near the front of the trailer. He pulled it into the cab and tossed it in the back.

"Smells nicer."

"I tried to air it out."

"Fatsy's a pig." He held out his hand for the keys. Other trucks started up along with theirs.

She didn't even notice when they got on the highway.

4

SEAGN WOKE UP WHEN THE SUNLIGHT HIT HER FACE as they crested a hill. She let out a moan that she didn't mean to utter. She saw Moose keeping his eyes on the road. His shoulders were slumped and he seemed to be barely awake. In the cup holder next to him sat a five-hour energy drink that wasn't there last night. Or early morning.

The dashboard said it was 8:30. Seagn yawned and Moose smiled at her, his eyes half-closed. "Enjoy your nap?"

"You've been driving all this time?"

"We're almost there."

The Ranch, right. In front of her was a tractor-trailer with the Tilt-A-Whirl on it.

She took a look in the mirror to find another semi behind them. "Convoy," she muttered.

"10-4 Rubber Duck."

She tilted her head in confusion.

"An old '70s song about convoys that my dad used to listen to on cassette."

They turned down a dirt road between some trees. After passing through a thick forest, they broke out into a large meadow. At the end of the meadow was a sheer drop into a huge pit where construction crews worked. No fencing or railings marked the boundary.

Moose pulled up to the edge of the forest, about fifty yards away from the rest of the trucks, and far away from Webby's RV. Men got out of the trucks — there were no women drivers, she noticed — and went to the RV. Some of the other trucks put up blinders in the front of their windows.

"Well, back to my crib," said Moose. "Gonna get some Z's."

He grabbed his bag and climbed — more like stumbled — down from the cab. Seagn followed him down on the passenger's side.

The meadow grass was more cushy than the grass in Salem Commons. Seagn walked to the back of the trailer, hearing the animals get excited as she walked by. She had to go to the bathroom, so she looked around for a portable toilet.

There weren't any. In fact, there were no amenities, just the meadow. No water, no sewer, no house … no nothing — except Webby's RV, the trucks, and a concrete-enclosed firepit.

Great, she thought, frowning. She went to the bathroom in the woods but felt exposed doing it.

After unlocking the trailer, she struggled to pull out the heavy tent. She slid it out, foot by foot, dragging it out of the trailer, letting it fall to the ground. Once she hauled the tent out, she stretched it by walking around it, tugging at the edges to stretch it out. The tent smelled wet and musty, and she hoped the sunny day would dry it out.

Suddenly, Seagn smelled bacon cooking, and her stomach rumbled. She hadn't had anything since a sausage and pepper sub sandwich the day before. Pancakes and bacon sounded awfully good right about now.

About a hundred yards away sat a fire pit, a few people gathered around it. A woman looked like she was cooking something on the open flame. Seagn salivated as she walked over to the fire pit. As she got closer, the smell of bacon got stronger. By the time she got there, she was famished.

The small group of people looked up at her. The woman with red hair who was cooking gave her a nod. "Hey."

"Hey," Seagn said. "Could you spare some food?"

"Ten dollars."

"Are you serious?"

"Yep. It's highway robbery, but we gotta make a living, too."

Seagn stormed back to the truck, dug out the ten, and brought it over. She got two barely-cooked pancakes and a side of three slices of bacon in exchange.

"Pleasure doing business. I'm Ruby."

"Shaun." She didn't have a fork, so she tore into the pancakes with her hands.

"This is Mark," she pointed to a rail-thin man with a baseball cap, who also nodded. "Carlos," another strapping young Hispanic man. "And Shayna."

The young girl next to Carlos nodded and waved. She looked a lot like Carlos, so Seagn assumed they were siblings.

"Hi," Seagn said. "I own the farm animals."

"It was a petting zoo until Fatsy got it." Ruby deftly flipped a pancake without a spatula. "He let it go to hell."

"I could tell. I have to get the sheep sheared; one of the goats has an ulcer or cyst; the horse needs new shoes —"

"Yeah, went straight to hell, like I said." Ruby gave her a look that said to Seagn, *Shut up, we don't care.*

Seagn ate quietly. Another couple showed up, this couple about her age, smiling and holding hands.

The man had a soldier's haircut and a severe face. The heavy-set woman's long blond hair was pulled up in a messy ponytail. Her horn-rimmed glasses were years out of style. The man assessed Seagn while he said, "Hey, Ruby, got any more flapjacks?"

"Yeah, I'll make some. Then the kitchen's closed. No more bacon, though."

The man shrugged, walked over to Seagn. "Hi, I'm Joe. This is Maggie."

Seagn wiped her hand on her pants and shook the man's offered hand. "Shaun."

"Nice to meet you finally. I heard you got the petting zoo."

"Yeah."

"Nobody goes to the petting zoo anymore," said Maggie. "Those poor animals."

"I'll bring them up to snuff," said Seagn. "They're hardy."

"They gotta be," Joe stated, glancing at Ruby making the pancakes. "They're from last year."

Ruby slid a pancake onto a paper plate. "I think Fatsy was hoping they died over the winter, but they didn't. You feed 'em, they're alive."

Seagn crunched into the bacon. "So, you just started?"

"This weekend was our first gig." Ruby poured the last of the batter into the pan and swished it around so that it covered the pan.

Joe took the cooked pancake. "You better take them outta that trailer or they'll destroy it."

"I assume I'm far away from everyone because of the smell?"

"Bingo."

"And the noise," said Maggie. "Is the rooster still there? Every fucking sunrise. Cock-a-doodle-doo!"

"I didn't see a rooster."

"Good. Hated that thing."

Ruby slid the cooked pancake around on the pan and flipped it. Carlos and Shayna wandered off to a car parked nearby.

"So, um … you all live here?"

Ruby gave her an angry look. "Yeah. You do too, bitch."

Seagn raised her hands in surrender. "I'm sorry —"

Joe snapped, "Jesus, Ruby, she's new."

"She's got the smell of some rich bitch on her," snapped Ruby, as she slid the pancake on the plate. "There. I'm fucking done. Make your own shit."

She gathered the hot pan, the bowls, and walked away into the forest. Mark hung his head and followed her.

"Don't mind her," said Joe. "She heard the rumor I did, that you paid cash."

"It was a cashier's check. I didn't mean to insult anyone."

"Well, you own the animals." Joe ate the pancake with his hands, too. "If you can pay people, that's a step above."

"Your tent got wet, huh?" Maggie said.

"Yes." Seagn glanced at the firepit. "Is this fire on all the time?"

"While we're here. There's only a dozen of us right now, but by the middle of the summer, this lot'll be full."

"Do you know how to cook?" asked Joe.

Seagn sighed. "I guess I'd better learn."

"You got a lot to learn, missy." Joe chuckled. "Especially if you're gonna be with us for the season."

"Yes, I've noticed that." She tossed her paper plate into the fire. "Well, back to work."

"Need help?"

"I don't know what I'm doing yet."

Joe glanced at Maggie, who shrugged. "You have to take the animals out of the trailer, let 'em do their shit, and keep 'em away from the rest of the people."

"How do I do that? It's not like I can put them on a leash and take them for a walk."

They laughed. "No, that's not it. C'mon. I'll show you."

"I assume I have to pay you?"

"*Pro bono*," he said. "First time's free."

•   •   •

With Joe's help, Seagn set up a corral with the aluminum fencing used for the pen set-up at Salem. That was fine and dandy, but the animals were looking for food. She set up troughs with food and water in strategic areas of the corral.

"That's the calmest I've seen 'em," said Joe while the animals jostled for food. "Them goats don't shut up."

Maisey stayed in the trailer, eating from the can of white sole that Seagn gave her. Maisey had presented her with two mice that morning.

"The goats are cute. But Tommy, I don't know about him." Tommy was at least standing up and eating, but he didn't eat much and lay back down almost as soon as he finished.

"You named 'em all?"

Seagn smiled and told him all their names. "Huey, Dewey, and Louie need a cut and a bath. That's what I'm going to do first."

"You know how to do that?"

"If I had the right tools. But I'm going to have to bring them somewhere."

"How? You can't keep bringing this truck everywhere."

"I know."

"You need a pickup truck."

That would be perfect: a small pickup, like a Ranger or a Tacoma. And if it could fit in the aisle of the trailer, that would be even better. Otherwise, she'd have to drive it with the convoy. Or she could tow it …

Joe clapped his hands in front of her face. "Hello?"

"Sorry, thinking."

"I could tell. Think you're all set now?"

"For now. Somehow I have to get to a grocery store."

"Me and Maggie are gonna go to Wal-Mart later."

"That sounds great. Do I pay you?"

"Gas money. You're getting the hang of it."

"Money talks around here," she said. Joe laughed again, walked across the field back to his "crib".

Now the animals, full and satisfied, gathered at the edge of the corral. Seagn squeezed her way by the fencing and pet the goats, scratched Bella's chin, and combed her hands through Shet's mane. Tiny rollicked in one corner; Sable on the other side nearest the trailer. The sheep kept eating grass, and Bob stayed to himself, surveying the rest of the animals as if he was in charge.

Seagn left the corral and went to the trailer. She pulled out her emergency vet kit, took out the small notebook, and started making a list for Wal-Mart.

•   •   •

After the jaunt to Wal-Mart, leaving there with over $400 depleted from her bank account, Seagn checked her balance at the ATM and was slightly shocked at how much money she had spent already. *It was to be expected,* she supposed.

She found out that The Ranch was located about ten miles north of Kittery, Maine. Checking on her phone, which was down to its last gasp of battery life, there were a few used-car lots in the area.

She knew they would treat her like she was stupid. And, in the world of cars and trucks, she really was. She'd have to bring a man with her, at least for looks. She wondered if Joe was available tomorrow to go truck shopping with her.

Seagn put away her groceries, which were mostly non-perishable items. She found herself buying her college comfort food of SpaghettiOs, canned ravioli, and ramen in a cup. She also had to purchase items that could be used on an open flame, such as a cast iron frying pan, an iron kettle, and oven mitts. Most importantly, she got her tea, small sugar packets, and a couple of boxes of tiny shelf-stable creamers.

Joe mentioned that she should go see Webby about her money. Webby paid in cash, all under the table, he said. You could ask for a "draw" — an advance on your pay, which he marked in a book and would deduct from the pay on Sunday.

So Seagn approached the RV. As she walked by one of the trucks, the back door opened, and Moose stood in the doorway.

"Hey," he called to her.

"Hey." She waved.

Moose yawned and stretched, his shirt riding up so she could see his abs and the treasure trail downward. She forced her eyes up to meet his face.

"What time is it?" he asked after completing his stretch.

"Just after one."

"Where you goin'?"

"I'm going to see Webby about my pay."

"Oh, good idea. And you owe me."

"I know."

She waited for Moose to jump down from the truck. He did, and stretched again. "Almost outta smokes," he muttered.

"That stuff will kill you."

"Yeah, yeah." He walked with her to Webby's place. "Hey, I have to go to get some breakfast — or lunch, as it is now. Wanna come for the ride? I have a helmet."

"What do I need a helmet for?"

"It's my motorcycle."

In all her life, she'd never ridden on a motorcycle. She thought they were dangerous and didn't trust them.

"It's just a rice-burner, not a Harley."

"Let me think about it, okay?"

He raised an eyebrow. But before he could say anything, Webby was already yelling at someone on the phone. Stephanie sat at the table, a cash box in front of her, and a pile of papers next to that.

"I suppose you're here for your money," she said, bored, as she flipped through the pages. "Sea-gan."

"Shaun."

"It looks like Sea-gan."

"My mother told me it's Gaelic. It's pronounced Shaun."

Stephanie shrugged. She counted out $120.

"That's it?"

"You closed early."

"But I opened it back up."

"Doesn't matter. People saw you closing so we took out that day's pay."

"Oh, my God, really?"

"That'll teach you not to close early."

"It was raining!"

Stephanie pulled out a sheet. "Sign here or give the money back and get the hell out."

Seagn angrily scribbled her name across the line on the bottom of the page.

Stephanie dismissed her by turning to Moose. "You drove?"

"Yes."

She pulled out his sheet, wrote down something on it. She counted out $275 for Moose and he wrote his name like a child trying out penmanship for the first time. Seagn couldn't see it, as the paper was whisked away.

"You owe me $35," said Moose as they walked back to the camping area.

She handed him $40. He gave her the five back. "I can't believe they took a day's pay out."

"Believe it. He's an asshole."

He followed her back to the trailer. "Want to help me with the tent?"

"Sure."

It was dry, so they folded it up.

"Ready for a bike ride?"

"I don't think so." Seagn brushed her hands against her jeans. "You go ahead."

"Suit yourself." He left.

Seagn got herself a bottled water and watched the animals. She had put a trough out for them and poured six gallons of water into it. They drank it all, so she refilled it. The animals were excited whenever she came near. Obviously more than just food.

She heard the rumble of a motorcycle and caught the tail end of Moose riding without a helmet into the forest.

Seagn spent the rest of the day examining the animals more closely. Most of them were healthy, if malnourished, though she knew their blood work would show other signs of neglect. She had to get the sheep sheared or they wouldn't be able to carry themselves. With the last of the gasoline, she ran the generator to charge up her phone.

Night came fast. The firepit lit up, and people gathered around it in the chill April air. Seagn decided to go make a visit.

Bundled up in blankets and seated on the grass, Carlos and Shayna gave her a nod. Ruby and Mark sat on lawn chairs, drinking huge bottles of beer. Maggie and Joe also sat on fancy folding chairs, drinking the Corona they got at Wal-Mart. Moose sat on the grass, smoking and flicking the ashes into the fire.

"So," said Ruby, "whatcha got?"

"Got?"

"For the party."

"This is a party?"

Ruby turned to Joe. "You didn't tell her to bring anything?"

"Forgot," said Joe, speaking through his nose, as he was smoking something that was not a cigarette. It smelled like skunk. "Let it go."

"Rich bitch better bring something next time."

Seagn stood steaming at the outskirts of the fire. "What do you want, Ruby? A cheese board? Maybe a wine tasting? I'll hire a classical music orchestra to come play, too."

Ruby drank deeply from her Colt 45. "Yeah, you can start with that shit."

"Ruby, stop being an asshole," said Moose. "She's not rich, or she wouldn't be here."

"You heard what she paid for that zoo."

Seagn leaned forward. "How much did I pay for it?"

"Ten grand. In cash."

"No. It was eight, and a cashier's check. I got the money from selling my parents' house on a lake in New York two years ago. My brother and I split the net after taxes and he's in school in Saracuse, while I finished veterinary school. There, you happy?"

"So you're a smart rich bitch."

"Let it fucking go," snarled Moose.

Ruby drank, saying nothing.

"Sit down." Moose patted the blanket next to him.

Thoughts flew through her mind. *Was he flirting with her? Was he going to try something?* She noticed that everyone seemed paired off — *was this expected?* She didn't know whether to trust the man with the long hair and broad shoulders who had been so kind to her. Was she supposed to give him sex in return?

She did sit down, but across from him. The ground was cold. She should have brought a blanket.

"I told you my life's story," she said. "How about yours?"

She looked to each one in turn. Mark was studying his bottle. Ruby gave her a glare.

Joe said, "I'll go."

Seagn sat back and waited.

"I was in the Army, and got discharged for conduct unbecoming."

"What did you do?"

"I don't want to talk about it."

Seagn glanced at Maggie. Maggie finished her Corona and reached for another one in the small cooler they had brought.

"Okay … how long have you been out of the military?"

"Three years now. Been working here for two of them. That's when I met Maggie."

Maggie gave them a small smile. "I worked in one of the vendors at the carnival — the cotton candy truck."

"Remember I bought so much cotton candy from you? Just so I could talk to you."

"You didn't eat it. You kept giving it away. I saw when you'd leave, you'd hand it to some kid."

"And when the carnival broke up, she came with me."

Seagn asked, "You live here?"

"We have a tent back there," he pointed past the trucks. "In the woods."

"You live here in the winter?"

"Nah, we go south."

"Florida," said Maggie. "We drive down there and back."

"I got family in Atlanta," said Joe. "Sometimes we stay there for a little while until we get on their nerves."

"Then we live in the car outside of Orlando, do some odd jobs here and there for gas and food."

Joe looked to Carlos. "What about you?"

He shrugged. His voice had a heavy Latino accent: "We came from Guatemala to get away from the drugs."

Unsaid, and known right there by Seagn, was that they were illegal aliens. Shayna didn't say anything. She only bundled up tighter in the blanket.

Seagn and the rest of them looked to Moose, knowing Ruby wasn't going to be forthcoming.

"Ran away to join the carnival when I was 17," he said. "Quit school and left home. Tried to get a regular job three years later, but I can't." He inhaled on the cigarette. "Nobody wants a high school drop-out."

"Yeah," said Joe as he sipped the Corona. "They're always lookin' for college kids."

Seagn shivered on the cold ground. "So, you're here. So, we're all here."

"Better get a blanket or you'll catch your death," said Maggie.

Moose snuffed out the cigarette. "You can have mine. I'm going to get something to drink, and I'll get another blanket."

"You got any Jack?" asked Joe.

Moose grinned, as he got up and gathered the blanket. "You read my mind."

"Great."

"Not too much," Maggie said.

"Why? We're not going anywhere for two more days."

Moose handed the blanket to Seagn. It was warm from his body heat and smelled like a man and burnt tobacco.

Seagn got up, spread it out, and sat on it while Moose went to his truck. The fire wasn't quite warm, but it was bright in the dark meadow.

"You gonna get a rooster?" asked Joe.

"No. You really can't pet a chicken. And they're prone to biting."

"Too bad. You could sell the eggs."

She sighed. *Did he know that roosters don't lay eggs?*

"It didn't look like there was any room for a chicken coop in the trailer." Seagn gathered the edge of the blanket and wrapped it around her back. "I suppose I could build one."

"You know how to do that?"

"No, but I can pay someone to."

Ruby snorted. "Rich bitch" was on the tip of her tongue, Seagn knew it. Moose returned with a bottle of amber liquid, and another blanket that he spread out on the ground. He cracked open the bottle and drank deeply, then passed it to Joe.

Joe took some, passed the bottle to Ruby, who gave it to Mark. Mark stared at it as if it was something strange, then lifted the bottle to his lips and drank, keeping an eye on Ruby. He passed it to Carlos, who passed it to Seagn. Seagn declined, giving it back to Moose.

"So," Seagn said. "What do you do around here?"

"Aren't you a chatterbox," Ruby snarled.

"I'm trying to find out what the right thing to do is."

"Right now, it's to shut up."

Joe waved a hand. "Don't mind her. She's just jealous."

"Fuck you, jealous." Ruby drank her beer. "I wouldn't want those fucking animals."

"No, but you were the 'rich bitch' last year with the fancy jewelry and all that shit." He craned his head. "Speaking of which, pawned it all off this winter?"

"None of your fucking business," Ruby snapped.

"Where's the car?"

"Webby said we can use the truck for driving around. It's free advertising."

"Nobody here wants Rockwell," Maggie said. "They want Ringling Brothers."

"You and Webby, huh?" Joe drank the amber liquid.

Ruby jumped out of her chair. "Fuck you." She grabbed her huge bottle of beer and folded up her chair. Mark silently folded up his chair as well and followed Ruby back to wherever their crib was.

Shayna said something in Spanish to Carlos, who nodded and replied. They moved into the prime spot that Ruby and Mark had vacated, next to Maggie and Joe, right in front of the firepit.

Joe stretched out his legs. "Now that she's gone, we can finally talk about her."

Moose shook his head, but Joe continued, "Yeah, she flaunted all her money. And Mark's money."

"Poor Mark," said Maggie. "I don't know what he sees in her."

"I think he's looking for a mother figure."

"Or he's getting beat up."

Everyone looked at Moose when he said that.

"Like verbally. She probably treats him like shit and he thinks that's what he is."

Asked Seagn, "Does he never talk?"

"Hardly ever," said Moose, sloshing the amber liquid around in the bottle. "You can never catch him alone except when he's working. She's always there, on top of him."

Carlos was speaking Spanish to Shayna, who nodded at some things. Seagn realized he was translating the conversation to her.

Seagn turned to her, now that she was sitting next to her, and smiled at her.

Shayna smiled back.

"Uh, *no habla Espanol.*"

Shayna laughed, sounding like a tinkling waterfall. "*Hablo.*"

"Oh. *No hablo Espanol.*"

She said something in Spanish and Carlos translated, "She says, 'Thank you for trying.'"

Seagn yawned. "I'd better get to bed. Now that I have clean sheets."

"Did you bomb that truck?" asked Moose.

"Like bug-bomb?"

"I would. Fatsy's a fucking pig."

Said Joe, "That's insulting the pigs. What's their names again? Tiny?"

"And Sable," said Seagn. "I might get a sow, then we might have piglets. But they reproduce very quickly, and I don't have the right environment for them."

"They need mud, right?"

"No. They're actually very clean. The mud is for when they're hot." Seagn got up and stretched, gathered the blanket and handed it to Moose. Moose shook it out, then folded it into a square. "Thanks for the blanket."

"You're welcome. Sleep well."

Seagn smiled at him, waved to the rest, who waved back, and she headed back to the trailer.

5

THE NEXT MORNING, Seagn fed the animals and Maisey, and ate some Pop-Tarts. Maisey hung around her while she struggled with re-arranging the pens to reflect the number of animals that she had. Most of the pen dividers were rusted or welded in place.

While she struggled with a rusted pen latch, Moose called to her. "What're you doing?"

She released the latch and kicked the fence. "Trying to move this."

"You probably need some WD-40." He climbed up into the trailer. "Let me take a look."

He came over to her and examined the latch. "Rusted really good in there. Definitely needs some grease."

"Do you have any?"

"No, but I can go get it. What else do you need from the store while I'm out?"

"More gas for the generator. Or a battery pack for my phone. I keep running it to charge my phone."

"You got a phone?"

"Doesn't everybody?"

He chuckled. "I sure don't. And Ruby charges by the minute."

"I'm sure she does."

He reached out and placed a hand on her arm. "Don't take it personal. Rule number one around here. Don't take anything anybody says personal."

Oh, no, he wants sex, she thought, and backed away. She struggled to say something other than her thoughts. "I thought Rule Number One was 'Money talks.'"

"That's definitely Rule Number One. Okay, so my rule is number two." He had taken back his hand, not looking as awkward as Seagn felt. "Be right back with the WD-40."

Seagn rubbed her arm where he touched it. *He wants sex, that's the only reason why he keeps coming around. I'm not giving it to him.* She shook her head while Maisey rubbed against her legs, looking for attention.

Seagn went to the generator and unplugged her phone. She used it to search for a farm that could do some sheep shearing. There were only two, so she called the first one on the list.

They told her that she'd have to bring the sheep to them. The second one said that, for an extra fee, they would go to her. Problem was, she had no idea where she was. Moose got back as she hung up the phone to the second farm. He pulled up in his motorcycle, which got the animals excited.

"Does this place have an address?" she asked Moose as he got off the bike.

"No idea. Why?"

"I need those sheep cut and I got someone to do it, but I don't know where we are."

"I can bring 'em here. Where's the place?"

She held out her phone and showed him a map. He scratched the back of his neck. "Um, I can't tell."

Seagn realized that Moose didn't know how to read a map.

"Maybe they know where Rockwell Carnival camps during the summer?"

"I didn't ask that."

"I can give them some landmarks with the directions."

She redialed and talked to the farmer. She put Moose on the phone who gave him directions like, "You know where the little red barn is on Route 1? Go about half a mile and you'll see a tar road …"

Seagn didn't pay attention, but Moose's directions seemed clear to the farmer, because he hung up soon after. "He'll be here in about an hour."

"Thanks."

"No problem. Now let's get this latch undone."

With the application of WD-40, and a lot of manhandling by Moose, the latch finally got loose. She moved the gate a couple of feet down the trailer.

"What are you doing this for?"

"I want to try and fit one of those little pickups in here."

He put his hands in his pockets. "I don't think it'll fit. Not with the animals, and this generator, and all the other shit you got packed in here." He pointed to the hitch on the trailer. "You can get another trailer for it."

"I might be a rich bitch, but I don't have unlimited funds. No, I have to fit it in here. Or maybe the VW."

"What VW?"

"My car back in Salem."

"A VW can't fit a pony in the trunk."

Seagn laughed at the vision that placed in her mind. "Or a cow. Yeah, I can see what you're talking about."

"I'll keep an eye out for a truck."

"Thanks, I appreciate it." She had her eye on another fence.

They got that one loose and placed it in the back at the same time a rumbling truck came into the field. The side of the light blue battered truck read "Morris Farms". Two men rode in the cab. They bounced their way toward Seagn's corral.

One man got out. "You Shaun?" he asked Moose.

"I am," said Seagn.

"Oh, sorry. I'm Jake." He held out his hand. Seagn shook it, and he held out his hand for Moose, who also responded. "This is my son, Junior. So, those the sheep?"

"Huey, Dewey, and Louie."

"Can they go up a ramp?"

"They go up the ramp into the trailer," Seagn said as they all approached the corral.

The goats, as usual, gathered at the entrance. Moose herded the goats away while Junior guided Dewey to the entrance. Jake set up a ramp onto the truck.

Junior and Seagn shoved the bleating sheep onto the truck, and so began the shearing with a huge electric razor. The sheep *baa*ed constantly, shaking and trying to get away. When the two men were done, Dewey looked like a big lamb.

"I'm probably going to have to wash before I card this wool," said Jake. "She hasn't been cut in years."

"At least," Seagn agreed. "I just inherited them."

They carried the sheep off the truck and worked next on Huey, then Louie. Again, they were girls, so Seagn had to rename them Blanche, Dorothy, and Rose. Seagn sighed as they drove away.

"I have to go check my balance."

"Want a ride?" Moose motioned to the motorcycle.

"No." She pulled out her phone.

"What are you afraid of?"

"They're not safe. A helmet isn't going to save me if I get thrown off it." Besides, there was nothing for her to hold onto, other than him.

"Suit yourself. I've been riding bikes since I was a kid."

She used the app on her phone to find out if there were any Primus ATM's in the area. She scratched at an itch on her back. "Anywhere I can take a shower?"

"Ruby has one. Costs five dollars for two gallons of water."

Unbelievable, she thought, *when a gallon cost at most a dollar each.* "Never mind."

"It's a sun shower. Warm water."

"I'll take my chances with the bottled water and some hand soap." She headed to the truck. "If you'll excuse me, I'd like a little privacy?"

"Sure," he said with a grin.

Seagn gave him a glare. He raised his hands in surrender, backed up to his bike.

•   •   •

Once I get everything settled, Seagn thought, *I'm going to rent a hotel room and take the hottest shower for an hour.*

She dumped the dirty water out of the truck, the only private place she could go, and then climbed down to the ground. Moose hadn't returned from his trip, so she decided to clean up the corral and throw the crap in the woods. The animals gathered around her — looking for food or attention, she wasn't sure. Bella licked her hair; Bob and Jack kept butting into her, almost throwing her off balance.

Moose finally returned with a roar of the bike. He parked near the trailer and watched as Seagn shoveled shit into the woods.

"Having fun?"

"Loads."

After Seagn finished, she washed her hands with the bottle of spring water and soap. Moose sat back on the bike and ate a sandwich he had gotten while he was out, while Seagn ate some cold ravioli out of a can — something she hadn't done since college.

"I can go with you to get a truck," said Moose, looking in the direction she stared at.

"I'm not riding on the back of that death machine."

Moose laughed and patted his motorcycle. "Hear that, honey? She called you a death machine. Now, that is a compliment."

Seagn frowned and ate.

"I know something about trucks. I can look under the hood and see if they're trying to pull one over on you."

She sighed. "Let me think about it."

"I'll go real slow. Like school-bus slow."

She looked at the motorcycle, then at the man who rode it. He wasn't going to give up the bike. She'd have to bite the bullet sometime.

But not right now.

•   •   •

This night, Seagn brought a bottle of wine and a blanket, and noticed Fatsy taking up most of the spot in front of the fire pit. She could smell the stench of bad weed coming off him.

Moose sat in his customary spot, while Ruby sat alone. Neither looked happy that Fatsy decided to join them. Next to him sat a skinny girl of about fourteen or fifteen, with brown hair pulled up in a ponytail. She wore boy shorts, with the firelight flickering off her tanned legs, and a short shirt, barely covering her budding breasts.

"Who're you?" she demanded, sipping from a bottle of what looked like wine cooler. "What's that you got there?"

"I'm Shaun. This," she held up the bottle, "is Riesling."

"Gimme here," she said, holding out a hand with a grasping motion.

"You're a little too young to drink this."

"Bullshit," she spat. "Gimme."

"Maybe if you ask nicely, I'll let you have a glass."

"Fuck the glass," said Fatsy. "It's fuckin' booze, ain't it? Give it over."

The two cups she had brought were obviously a waste, as she handed the bottle of white wine to Fatsy. He cranked it open and took a swig, then spit it out. "Fuck is this shit!"

The girl laughed and swiped the bottle out of Fatsy's hand. She also took a swig; the look on her face was of obvious disgust. "Ugh, this is horrible!"

She shoved it at Seagn, who took the bottle, and poured the white wine on the ground. "First, you're not supposed to chug it down. This wine is too sweet for that."

"That's not fucking wine," said the girl, and held up her long-necked bottle. "This is wine. Right, Uncle Fatsy?"

"Wine for girls," he said, spitting. "Gah, I need something to take the taste out of my mouth."

The girl offered her bottle, but he refused, instead taking out another joint. He used the fire to light it, leaning dangerously close. Moose looked for a minute like he was going to give Fatsy a shove into the flames. Seagn smiled, visualizing that.

Fatsy sat back, and the girl kicked sod into the fire, giggling at the moist grass hitting the embers.

"What's your name?" Seagn asked.

"Alison." She drank and threw the empty bottle into the fire. It didn't shatter but the firepit hissed. "Shaun is a boy's name."

"It's actually a unisex name."

Alison roared. "She said 'sex'!"

Fatsy leered at Alison. "Yep, she did."

Seagn's stomach roiled. Moose jumped up. "I gotta go."

"I think one of the animals needs me."

"I'll bet," said Fatsy, still smoking. Ruby looked helpless.

"I'll walk you back to the trailer," Moose said.

"How chivalrous of you."

Moose leaned in close, smelling of cigarettes and Jack Daniels. "I'm going to punch that pig in the fucking snout if I see him do that again." Then he leaned up and started walking to the trailer.

Seagn said quietly, "He's been doing that all night?"

"All night," said Moose.

"Is he Webby's brother?"

"No. She calls him Uncle because him and Webby are friends."

"Unbelievable. To think, I'm sleeping in that, that …"

"Told you, you should have bug-bombed it."

"I'll wash the whole truck down with bleach tomorrow."

Moose laughed.

"You think I'm kidding?"

"Do you have bleach?"

"You'll have to go get it for me."

"Oh, so I'm your errand boy?"

She batted her eyes at him. "Could you get some for me?"

He laughed again. "With those pretty eyes, I can't say no."

She hoped that he didn't see her blush. "I'll get some money for you."

"Okay."

Seagn didn't expect him to say, *Don't worry about it,* since she knew how much he made and how many hours he worked. This downtime was not paid for. She got out $20 and handed it to him from the cab of the truck. "I'm going to bed."

"I'll get what I can carry for you tomorrow."

"Keep the change."

Moose gave her a sketchy salute and left her there.

She refused to sleep in the cot. She slept sitting up in the passenger's seat instead.

•　　　•　　　•

The next day, Seagn got the bleach and washed down everything. It took her most of the day after feeding the animals.

Moose was busy for the day, starting up all the trucks and testing out all the generators. He showed up at her trailer with three full gas tanks and said, "Sixty dollars, please."

"How much a gallon?"

"It doesn't matter. That's what Webby wants."

"God," Seagn spat, and retrieved the cash.

"Pleasure," Moose said with a smile, pocketing the money. "If you had your own truck, you wouldn't pay crazy prices."

"I get the point. Money doesn't grow on trees. I checked my balance this morning and it's going down pretty fast."

"Can't you borrow from your brother?"

"He needs it for engineering school."

"More like booze and girls," said Moose. "At least that's what I would do if I was in college."

"You're not Liam." *In a way, thank God.*

"Mmhmm." He walked back to Webby's trailer.

A couple of hours later, Moose came back with Webby in tow. "What happened to the sheep?"

"They were carrying too much wool, so I had to shear them."

"They don't look like sheep."

"Give them time. It'll grow back."

Webby leaned precariously on the temporary fencing. The animals came up to him. He looked like he wanted to kick them away.

"Well, they look better."

"It helps if you feed them right and give them the attention and caring that's expected."

Webby scoffed. "Yeah, right."

The truck roared to life on the opposite end of the trailer. Seagn turned in that direction. "What's that?"

"Moose is checking out the truck, make sure it starts and can move. You gotta be ready to move tomorrow morning. We're going to Worcester."

"So, I pack them in tonight?"

He shrugged. "Do it at two in the morning, I don't care. Just be ready for eight."

"What happens at Worcester?"

"Same shit, different spot. You get the usual." He turned to face her. "What's this I hear you're buying a truck?"

"Just one of those little pickups to carry feed."

"Where you gonna put it?"

"I think I'm going to end up driving it."

"Gonna put a lot of miles on that if you do, goin' from here to gigs. And who's driving it?"

"Me."

Again, Webby scoffed. "Yeah. Right."

He walked away before Seagn could come up with something to say. She ended up kicking the fencing and the goats jumped away like frightened cats.

Loading up the animals that night was just as easy as it had been before. She gave them new bedding, and Maisey slept with her in the cab.

The next morning, at sunrise, Seagn saw about a dozen or so people drive in with different cars and motorcycles, even bicycles and mopeds. Some were dropped off; others left their modes of transportation parked in the meadow and checked in with Webby. Most of them were men, looking ragged and rough around the edges. Moose came over to her trailer.

"Where did all these people come from?" she asked.

Moose looked back at the gathering of people near Webby's trailer. "They work for the carnival. Sometimes we pick up people at the spots for day labor, but most times we hire 'em for the season and they come here to jump off."

Seagn didn't ask what "jump off" meant, but assumed it was to leave from The Ranch.

"Better watch out for some of them. Keep your money close or hide it really well. Lock the door in the truck, too, because they'll take your shit and sell it."

"Okay," Seagn said.

The trucks started at eight on the dot. Seagn tested the lock on the back of the trailer; found it secure. The animals were settled down, ready for the long ride to Worcester.

6

MOOSE SEEMED TO LIKE CLASSIC ROCK, so switched the stations around, gaining and losing them as they moved through broadcast zones. Seagn missed satellite radio, where she could listen to *No Shoes Radio* — modern and some classic country.

"Where are you from, anyway?" asked Seagn about ten miles out.

"Woonsocket," he said. "Rhode Island."

"Is that where you went to school?"

"Yeah, I had special classes."

"Oh?"

"Vocational training. I learned how to fix engines." He glanced at her. "What about you? Lived in Salem all your life?"

"My parents were from upstate New York. I moved to Salem after getting a job at the clinic."

"They didn't need vets in upstate New York?"

"No, not that. I went to school in Boston and they were advertising."

"Your parents died?"

"Yeah. During the Pandemic."

"Oh, sorry."

"It's okay. Thank you."

He nodded. "Nasty bug, that. Put us out of business for over a year."

She never had it and got the vaccine every year to make sure she didn't. She remembered her mother's face when they had FaceTimed goodbye, and she resolved to never put her brother through that situation again.

"Did you get it?" she asked.

"Nope. Couldn't work that year, so I was living with my step-sister. Had to do shit around the house. My nieces got it though. They're okay."

"That's good."

"What's veterinary school like?"

"You're very busy. You have to examine and memorize all kinds of animals' physiology. But they never taught us to deal with pet parents."

"You mean the owners?"

Seagn chuckled. "Yeah. They should have a class on human psychology and dealing with people."

Moose changed lanes as he talked. "It's on-the-job training. Like here. You gotta deal with some crazy people. I was running the motorcycle ride and some father wanted to put their six month old on the bike. They can't even sit up straight, or hold the handlebars. I had to tell him no, and he got Webby, who told him he had to sign a waiver in case his kid fell off." Moose shook his head. "Webby never says no. Customer is always right."

"Did he put the kid on it?"

"Yeah, with the father on the bike, too. Looked fucking stupid. I cut it short. You seen the bike ride? They're little bikes, for kids. When you hit 16, you shouldn't ride it. You're too big. But we get some people who are just fucking stupid."

"Maybe they never rode a motorcycle."

"Or they're too scared. Hey, if I'm manning the ride, I'd let you go on it. You can get some practice."

Seagn laughed. "Gee, thanks."

After two hours of driving, they pulled over into a truck stop to get gas. Seagn got some candy while the rest of the caravan went to the bathroom or refilled their gas tanks. Seagn waited until the crowd thinned out before going to the bathroom. The woods had been cleaner than these bathrooms.

She nearly retched while washing her hands in the dirty sink. Bolting from the bathroom, she ran back to the truck and took out some wipes to wash her hands instead.

"Not exactly the best truck stop," said Moose, getting into the cab. "But at least the toilets flush."

"They're disgusting." Seagn handed a wipe to Moose. He took it without saying anything.

"Some are a lot worse," he said, as he pulled into his spot in the convoy, between the ferris wheel and the fried dough truck. "I mean a *lot* worse."

"I don't want to know."

"None of the truckers use this one because it's off the beaten path and cheaper than the ones on I-90. We usually hit this place on the way to points west."

"How far west do you go?"

"West Springfield was the farthest I've gone, but that was a couple of years ago. Too rich for my taste."

"Do you go to Connecticut?"

"Right before New York once. Last year, I think. I don't know if we're going there this year."

Seagn ducked a hand in the glove box and pulled out the paper that Stephanie had copied for her. "It looks like just a few stops here and there, all over New England."

"That changes. We could go to a spot in Mass, and another one in Vermont the next week. Sometimes two spots at the same time. Some spots only have room for a couple of rides, or the bouncy-house crew gets called in for a private party."

"You do private parties, too?"

"Anywhere Webby can make money."

"You know," Seagn said, putting the paper back. "Why do you call him Webby?"

Moose smiled. "His last name is Webster. Almost everybody gets a nickname. Fatsy, Steph, Alley, the Mick —"

"And what's your real name?"

"You know what they say about real names."

"No, I don't."

"They have power over people. I don't answer to that name no more, anyways. Just Moose."

"How did you get that name?"

He shrugged. "No idea. Somebody started calling me that and it stuck. The best thing to do, if someone gives you a nickname — so long as it ain't 'bitch' or 'slut' or anything like that — is to take it."

"So 'smart rich bitch' is out?" She grinned at him.

He chuckled. "Definitely out."

The exits started showing signs of crossing into Massachusetts and, a half hour later, they had crossed the border and picked up I-90 to Worcester.

•   •   •

"A parking lot," Seagn said, as they chugged up the hill to the opening of a warehouse club.

"A big parking lot. We could set up a pro football game in here."

"I have to set hay down for the animals."

"And clean it up."

"Isn't that just a joy."

Moose parked at the furthest edge of the parking lot, which faced a fenced-in vacant lot that was under construction for yet another big box store. The trucks came into the lot, parking at different sections, and, Seagn noticed, blocking her off.

"Where am I going?" Seagn asked.

"Ask Webby," Moose said. "All I know is I always park away from the midway."

Seagn got down off the truck, leaving Maisey inside the cab. Moose left and disappeared among the workers. Seagn stormed up to Webby and Steph, setting up their RV.

"Okay, where do I go?"

"Between the Tilt-a-Whirl and the swings."

Seagn glanced in the direction of the two rides. It was a ten-by-six area, even with the trucks parked there.

"You gotta wait 'til they're done setting up," Webby said. "Then squeeze in there."

"Seriously? I don't have enough room for the tent."

"Fuck that, then, I don't give a flying fuck." Webby glared at her. "All you do is fucking complain. I don't know why you're still with us. I thought you'd take these animals to some sanctuary farm and save us the trouble."

"One, because people don't see farm animals every day and they're a novelty. Two, because I know these animals will be healthy specimens in time. Three, I complain because I have the animals' best interests in mind. And four —"

"Just do it," Webby snapped, walking away. "Make sure they don't stink up the place."

Seagn glanced at Steph, who also turned around and walked into the RV.

"Hell," she grumbled, going back to the trailer. She unlocked it and took out the ramp.

Watching the carnival get set up was amazing to her. The rides rose from their positions; the tents for the fair seemed to just appear, with the middle tent pole going up first.

Someone else pulled into the parking lot — a black trailer towed behind a white truck. The black trailer had emblazoned in yellow lightning font on the side, "The Amazing Tightrope Walker." Beneath that was "Walked between the Twin Towers."

Seagn sat and waited for the Tilt-a-Whirl's fences to get set up, then she pulled out her own. She had to carry them a good fifty feet to the area to set up her boundaries. When all was said and done, she had enough room probably for the goats and the cow.

Bella would be a novelty; she was friendly and liked to lick hands, which would make the kids giggle. The goats were active and cute. The sheep were upset that they got sheared, so they were milling about like pouting old ladies. Shet wasn't ready to ride yet, as she had to get his shoes fixed. And the pigs — well, she didn't have room for them and didn't know if they would be interesting enough to people.

She lay down some hay from a bale that she had bought from Wright's. Setting up the tent was going to be impossible. She looked at the fencing and the two pens, trying to think of where to put the rigging for the tent. She couldn't tie it to the temporary fencing, and she couldn't hammer the stakes into the asphalt.

Fatsy came over to see the empty pens. "Where's the animals?"

"In the trailer. I'll take them out when we start the carnival. It's not starting today, is it?"

"Not 'til tomorrow at five. They better be ready. How come you only got two?"

"That's all the room I have."

"You can squeeze them in there."

"I'm not going to because they have no room to lie down."

"Who cares?"

Seagn whirled and glared at Fatsy. "I do."

Fatsy backed up a step. "Jesus, you don't have to get all huffy."

"I know you and Webby don't care about the well-being of animals, but I'm a vet and I do care. I have one sick goat that I'm nursing back to health because of your neglect. If I wanted to make your life miserable, I'd report you to the SPCA."

Fatsy blinked, backing away. He turned and left, yelling at the guys setting up the Swinger.

"Damn right, you better run," Seagn muttered. She should report him. But she wanted to give him more rope to hang himself.

She was still preparing the pens for the goats and Bella when Moose came over. "Hey, the store isn't open until tomorrow's grand opening. Want me to get you a grinder?"

"What would I do with a — what?"

Moose waved his hand. "Sub. Sandwich. We call them 'grinders' in Woonsocket."

"Oh, sure. Yes. Tuna with pickles. Large. I'm starving."

"You got it."

She thought he had brought the motorcycle, so was surprised to see him start walking alone down the hill.

"Hey, wait!"

He turned.

"I'll come with you." She locked the trailer door and jogged up to him. She patted her pocket to make sure the key and money were in there and fell into step next to him.

"I thought you'd be bored to hell with me by now."

"No, I'm not." She smiled. "I'm really not."

"Good." He put out his hand.

Klaxons rang in her head. *Omigod, omigod, he wants to hold my hand, omigod where does this go from here?*

She stopped, stared at his hand.

He took it back, blushing. "Sorry."

"No, I — no. It's, it's okay."

He started walking away. She mentally slapped herself.

At the bottom of the hill was a small strip mall with a Subway and a Bank of America ATM. Across the street was an Applebees and, next to that, a J.D. Byrider.

"Let's go to Applebees," Seagn said. "Do we have enough money for that?"

"Depends. What're you drinking?"

"Just soda. I have my phone, so I can pay for it. I owe you for all the errands you've done for me."

"Then dinner at Applebees it is."

•   •   •

Since the Pandemic, restaurants had to rescale to meet the new social distancing requirements. Instead of closing and remodeling, most restaurants blocked off booths next to each other. When they walked in, they saw some booths taped off. The waiting area had three people in it.

Following the social distancing rules, Moose and Seagn stood on the opposite side of the party of three, maybe about four feet away. A hostess came and got the party, returned to clean the seats with a disposable wipe.

"Two?" she asked as she finished.

"Yes," both of them said at the same time.

"Bar or booth?"

"Booth, please?" said Seagn.

The hostess glanced at her tablet that showed where people sat She touched an area twice, picked up another pair of tablets about five-by-seven in size and said, "Right this way."

They followed her to an area two booths away from the emergency door. Moose let Seagn get in first, and the hostess handed the tablets to them. "Lara will be your waitress."

They both nodded as the hostess turned away from them, her job done.

"Well, that was interesting," said Moose. He perused the menu, swiping right as he turned the pages on the tablet.

"They look like they're busy." Seagn looked up from the menu to take a gander around.

"So do I have a budget?"

"Get what you want."

Lara, a rotund bleached-blond woman with dark roots showed up at their table. "What can I getcha?"

Moose looked up. "What do you have on tap?"

"Sam Adams, Bud, Guinness, some IPA —"

"Sam Adams."

Lara nodded, bored. "And you?"

Seagn glanced at the menu. "Just a Coke."

"Pepsi okay?"

"Mountain Dew, then."

"Sure." Lara headed to the bar.

"You're not going to get to sleep if you drink Mountain Dew," Moose said.

"I hate Pepsi. It's too sweet."

"I can't tell the difference. Dark soda is dark soda."

"There's definitely a difference."

Seagn made her decision and put the tablet down. Moose was still looking through the menu when Lara returned.

"Have you decided?"

Seagn nodded. "I'll have the coconut shrimp basket with cheese fries."

"Bacon?"

"Why not."

"And you, sir?"

Moose frowned. "It's either the ribs or the buttered steak."

"I'd go with the ribs," said Lara. "Full rack?"

"Sure. Stuffed baked potato with all the fixings."

"Soup or salad?"

"I don't want either of them."

Said Seagn, "I'll have his salad. Blue cheese."

Lara nodded. "I'll put this right in."

She left, taking the tablets with her. Moose looked around, folding his hands in front of him on the table. Seagn stared at his hands, big and broad — workman's hands. Hers were chafed due to the alcohol baths and constant hand washing.

"So," she said, his action earlier bothering her. "Um, I didn't mean to … to insult you."

"What do you mean?"

"I didn't take your hand."

He smiled. He didn't have dimples, but he did have a nice smile. Why was she being so hard to get?

"It's okay. I thought I was being pushy."

"I just … I —" She bit her bottom lip. "How do I put this?"

"You want to stay chaste and celibate for the right person. I get it."

"No, that's not it —"

"You want to be fast and easy, then?" Moose raised both eyebrows.

"NO!" Seagn's face reddened.

He laughed. "I'm kidding with you."

She looked down at her hands, waiting for the heat in her face to stop pulsing.

"Something happened. Almost married?"

"No. I had a bad breakup recently."

"He stalk you?"

"I worked with her."

She didn't look up at him, knowing that he would give her a shocked look, hidden by a deep drink of the beer that appeared just in time.

"Oh. Well, that explains —"

"No, it doesn't." She examined a tear in the tablecloth near his hands. "I—I've been with men and women. Right now, I don't want to get distracted."

"From?"

Now Seagn looked up at him. "Taking care of the animals."

His beer was half finished. That must have been some shock.

"Married to your job. Yeah, I can get that. Well," he said, leaning back, "I like animals too."

"Then why didn't you do anything when Fatsy took care of them?"

He looked at the beer, grabbed it, and then drank the rest of it down like it was ginger ale. "You know how things work around here."

"No, I don't. Fatsy's just like everyone else."

"He's not. He's Webby's butt-buddy. You cross him, you get a rough life here in Rockwell." He waved to Lara, who nodded and went to the bar. "Why do you think you got such a small spot?"

"Fatsy?"

"Wouldn't doubt it."

"Fatsy told me to shove them all in that spot. There's no room."

"And you told him, 'Yes, sir'?"

"No, of course not."

"Bad move. Webby will be on your ass like flies on shit."

A second beer arrived. Lara took the empty glass. "Your food will be up soon."

"I don't need Webby to tell me what to do." Seagn raised her head. "Look. I left that kind of place already. I don't need to get out of one authoritarian workplace into another one."

He raised his glass. "Welcome to the carnival, where the almighty dollar is supreme." He drank. "If Webby thinks he's losing money, he'll cut you off. And then what will you do? Can you put the goats in your apartment in Salem?"

"My landlady probably would let me," she said. "Though I doubt it's zoned for farm animals."

Moose chuckled. "Fatsy's the supe, so we do what he says. Even if it's wrong."

"I'm not going to surrender to him."

"Okay, what about compromise?"

"What do you mean?"

"There's an empty spot between some of the rides. What if you fit them there?"

"Between what rides?" She drank.

"Next to the sit-and-spin and the baby train."

"Will he let me?"

"If he wants all the animals out, tell him that you have to have two areas."

"I'll have to look at the size of —"

"You really enjoy making things difficult," he said crossing his arms and sitting back.

The food arrived before she could retort. Seagn looked down at her shrimp and was able to count the number of them on one hand. There were more fries than shrimp and a strange orange-yellow dipping sauce in a small bowl next to the shrimp. Moose's baby-back ribs were placed on a smaller plate, to give the illusion that the rack was huge. His overloaded baked potato was on a separate plate, and a small bowl of barbecue sauce came with it.

"Everything good?"

"Fine," said Seagn.

"Yeah," said Moose.

Lara gave them that tired smile and left.

Moose leaned in. "I think we got fucked over here."

"Remind me not to come here for dinner tomorrow."

"Costco will be open. Maybe we can get free pizza slices." Moose pulled a bone off the ribs, leaving the meat behind.

"I'm not — am I really making things difficult?"

"You're backtalking the boss and his assistant. What do you think?"

"They're ordering me to do things."

"Because that's what they're used to doing. Most of the guys are junkies or dropouts like me. We need to be told what to do." He ended up using a fork and knife to eat. "What you need to do is prove that you don't need to be told what to do. They want the animals out, you put them out. Every time."

She dunked the shrimp into the dipping sauce and made a face after tasting it. It was mango: too sweet, and disgusting.

They ate in relative silence, commenting on the lack of quality in the food. For what she was paying, she should have at least had ten shrimp instead of five "jumbo" shrimp and a pound of fries. Moose was disappointed as well. Seagn left a low tip for Lara and vowed never to return.

As they walked back up the hill, they couldn't talk to each other because of the intensity of the climb. They got to the top, and everything in the carnival remained dark. The only light was a pair of spotlights shining upward to the sky.

Seagn went to the RV as Moose separated from her to go somewhere else.

"Webby?" called Seagn.

"Yah?" Webby peered out of the screen door. "Whachu want now?"

"Fatsy wants me to put all the animals out, but I need another spot. Can I go next to the kiddie train?"

Webby opened the door and stepped outside. Seagn pointed in the dark. She couldn't see the area clearly but assumed she could fit the sheep and Shet there. The pigs, well … not this time around.

"I guess."

There was no way Webby could see where she was pointing.

"I'll set it up tomorrow."

"'kay." Webby dipped back into the RV.

Seagn turned around and bumped into a large black man that she hadn't met before.

"'scuse me," he said, his voice deep with a twang to it.

"Sorry," she said.

"Webby in?"

"Yes."

"Is he in a good mood?"

"I couldn't tell."

The man laughed, like a rolling drum. "You can tell, believe me, you can tell."

"He didn't yell at me."

"Then he's in a great mood." He opened the temporary gate and stepped into the RV's area. "If you'll excuse me."

Seagn watched the man glide into the area and knock on the metal part of the screen door.

Webby's voice came out of the RV, "Jesus fucking Christ, now what?"

Not so much in a great mood, Seagn thought, as she bolted back to the trailer.

•　　•　　•

Animals fed and bedded down for the night, Maisey curled up in her lap, Seagn sat on the edge of the trailer looking out at the vacant lot across from her. At this time tomorrow, the carnival would be in full swing. Right now, however, it was dark and lonely.

I shouldn't have told Moose about the Ex, Seagn thought. She didn't want to call that woman by name anymore. Like Moose said, names have power. And anyone with her name would forever remind her of the intense three months of bullshit and high-maintenance that she had to go through.

Moose was handsome enough. He probably wasn't high maintenance. But she worked with him. It would be awkward — again. Not worth it.

She set Maisey down, locking her in the trailer with the animals. She went to sleep on the cot, hearing "Bad Romance" in her head.

•　　•　　•

Herding the goats fifty yards to their spot was like herding cats in the veterinary office. She tried treats, but they didn't get the hint. She ended up using a broom as a guide.

Tommy looked better and was eating again. The rest of the goats pranced and tried to escape, so she had to give them gentle taps to guide them toward the Tilt-A-Whirl. She knew she looked amusing because she could see people watching her and laughing.

After getting them into the pen, they looked to her for treats. She gave them each one handful of food, and then went back for Bella.

The crowd that had gathered was disappointed in seeing her with the come out with the cow. They dispersed, so she could get the sheep out. They didn't try to escape like the goats. Shet was tranquil when she led him to his pen.

And so, her animals were out. She had to keep an eye on both places, about thirty yards apart. The store opened at high noon, and the parking lot that hadn't been taken up by the carnival was full. The blue ticket booth had a sign across it, "Free rides until 5 pm."

The carnival was bustling until then. People pet the goats through the fencing, got licked by Bella, patted Shet, and didn't know what to make of the sheep who gathered in the corner. Seagn walked back and forth, cleaning their shit with a broom and bucket.

During the day, the tightrope walker set up his display. He tied a tall, thin pole to the trailer and set up a rope that went directly across to the roof of the wholesale club. The rope was barely visible, not even as wide as a phone cable.

Seagn didn't get to watch much of the high-wire act, concentrating on the animals and keeping the area clean. At five, the ticket booth opened, the spotlights and ride lights came on, and the carnival became the hot spot. Seagn couldn't help but smile at the kids running every which way, how they were mesmerized by the size of Bella compared to the goats.

The animals looked to the people for food, so Seagn had an idea. *If I prepare a bag of food and sell it for a quarter or fifty cents, and give it to the kids, they can feed the animals.* Then she wouldn't have to do it at the end of the night.

Maybe tomorrow, she thought.

By closing time at nine, she was tired. She had to guide the animals in the dark back to the trailer, feed and bed them down. She brought the goats two by two, as that was easier for her to handle.

After she finished, Moose came over to her with a "Hey", with Joe and Maggie in tow. "We're going in town, see if they rolled up the sidewalks or not. Want to come?"

Seagn locked up the trailer and leaned against it. Her better angels wanted her to get some sleep.

"Sure," she said.

Moose beckoned, and they went to Joe's car. Moose squeezed into the back with Seagn. Sitting down was a bad idea, as the rocking motion of the car made her drowsy.

They drove past the Applebee's and a car lot. Seagn thought she saw a couple of small trucks there but didn't get to see them clearly in the dark. Past both was a series of strip malls and KFC, McDonald's, Burger King, and Taco Bell. Past that cluster of fast-food joints was another strip mall with a bar in it. They pulled into the crowded parking lot.

"Good enough for me," said Moose, getting out.

Joe nodded. "As long as they have Jack, it's good enough for me too."

People stood outside smoking, some with drinks in their hands. Moose nodded to them as if he knew them and held the door open for the group to go in.

Definitely a bar, a hopping one at that, with loud music coming from speakers everywhere around them. Seagn could hear the noise of a pool break and turned her head toward the pool tables. All of them were taken.

"What'll it be?" asked the bartender when they got there. Seagn had to yell for her soda, not trusting the alcohol to keep her awake.

"Put some rum in it," said Moose. "I'll buy."

The bartender looked to Seagn, who shrugged, and put her phone away.

"Relax," he said, handing her the rum and Coke, while he held a mug of beer.

"That's the problem. I might fall asleep standing up."

"You get used to it."

"Lack of sleep?"

"And the hard labor. I saw you with those goats. Why didn't you ask for help?"

"Everyone seemed to be busy."

"If you paid more than Webby, they'd come to work for you."

"I can't. I'm running out of money. I have to get more feed and I really need to get something that takes me places, something with a heavy-duty trunk."

"There's that car lot near the spot," said Joe. "Maybe you can go there at lunch or something and you can take a look."

"I won't have time to go down the hill and come back."

The group fell silent, letting the loud music wash over them. Seagn used the free Wi-Fi to check her emails.

Liam sent his weekly update; her Ex had sent an email, too. She deleted it with the normal run of junk and scams.

The bartender placed another drink in front of her. "From the gentleman over there."

She looked around to the corner of the bar to see a bald man raise a glass to her, giving her a wink and a smile. She pushed it away. "Give it back to him."

"You might not want to do that."

"Is he the owner? The manager? Some Mafia kingpin?"

"No, no, and maybe."

Seagn shook her head. "Not interested, sorry. Tell him that."

Moose saw the bartender walk away and leaned to her ear, "Anything wrong?"

"I can take care of it," she said.

The Mafia kingpin stepped away from the bar when the bartender went to talk to him. She watched out of the corner of her eye that the man was headed her way.

Moose saw him too and stepped in front of Seagn. She held her breath.

The man gave Moose a nod and kept on walking. She couldn't see Moose's face, but she got a sense that he was staking out territory. She didn't know whether to feel flattered or insulted.

Moose turned to her. "Everything okay?"

She sipped her drink, tasting more Coke than rum. "Were you going to do anything?"

"I just did."

Joe smiled and said, "That's Moose's 'Don't Fuck With Me' aura in action."

Seagn couldn't tell in the dim light if Moose was blushing or not, but he did offer her a small smile and bent his head to the beer.

"And you do not want to fuck with Moose," said Maggie with a laugh. She sipped from a neon-green drink with an umbrella in it.

"One time," Joe began, "remember that place in Wareham? Some guy threw a punch at Moose and he just picked him up and threw him into a car, right?"

Moose indeed was blushing.

"Alarm blaring and all that shit!"

Seagn smiled. "So you get into fights?"

"I try not to," he muttered.

"That's the aura, man," said Joe. "You turn that on and if somebody's gonna fuck with you, they get *hurt*."

"So noted," said Seagn, sipping her drink again. She didn't much care for it, so she put it down on the bar and turned away from it.

"We don't need to rehash old war stories," said Moose.

"They're so fun, man! You and Al, man, you guys got into some trouble. I wonder what Al's up to now?"

"Hopefully not chained to a wife, kids, and a job. You know how he was."

Joe raised his beer. "Freedom! Living off the grid. Cash only."

"A militia-man."

"If only he'd put down the pipe, he could have gotten in the Army."

"He didn't really want to serve. Didn't trust the government."

Seagn let them talk among themselves and gazed at herself in the mirror across from her at the bar. The Mafia kingpin had disappeared into the crowd. She felt out of place, not wanting to be here. She wanted to be back at the trailer, asleep. Or even home.

She took out her phone and wondered how to reply to Liam. *I took out some money and bought animals for a traveling side show,* she thought, as she stared at Liam's letter without reading it. *I'm nursing them all back to health. I quit my job and I'm living in a truck. All good. Luv you.*

Seagn put the phone away. The other three still chattered between themselves. Joe and Moose had a refill of the beer, and Maggie was still working on the green drink, though she laughed a lot louder than some of the people in the room. Seagn sighed, took out her phone again, scrolling through Facebook. She started deleting friends from work.

"What's so important?" asked Joe, putting a hand in front of Seagn's phone.

"My brother," she said, putting the phone away, glaring at Joe. "I'm using the Wi-Fi here to check my emails."

"Is that the brother that you split the money with?"

"Yes. He's just checking in."

"You gonna get more animals?" asked Maggie.

"I don't know yet. I have to get the ones I have healthy."

"Chickens," said Moose.

Joe scoffed, "No way! They shit everywhere."

"How about a snake?"

"Farms don't have snakes"

"Sure they do."

"You're thinking pythons, right?"

Moose shrugged. "It's gonna be a petting zoo, isn't it? What about petting snakes?"

Seagn said, "I'm not getting a snake."

"Don't like snakes?"

"Not particularly. But if it gets out, it'll be hard to find. And no, pythons are not on farms."

Joe said, "You could dance with it, Shaun!"

Seagn sighed, pushed past Moose and headed for the door. She thought she could hear Joe say, "What?" as she went by.

The air was cool and crisp, and she hadn't brought a jacket. She stepped to the opposite side of the smokers, hugged herself to keep warm. She looked for the Mafia kingpin but didn't see him outside. At least that was taken care of.

Moose came out soon after with Joe and Maggie.

"I'm sorry," said Seagn. "I shouldn't have come. I'm tired."

Joe shrugged. "It's okay. It's your first gig."

"We can go back," said Maggie.

"I don't want to ruin your evening."

Moose shrugged. "I got my beer. I'm cool."

"Yeah, we're all set to go back." Maggie led the way to the car.

•   •   •

Seagn heard the rain hitting the roof of the truck as she turned over in the cot. She slept in her clothes now because it was cold, easier to get in and out of bed. However, she knew she needed to change out of yesterday's clothes. At least the underwear and her shirt.

In the cab of the truck, she changed clothes, then took down the shade over the windshield. Rain was coming down in sheets in the dawn. Her phone said it was 6:30. The carnival — the store — was going to open at nine.

Checking her phone for the weather, it said it was going to rain all day. She should have checked yesterday. Now she was going to deal with a leaking trailer tarp, wet hay out in the temporary pens, and miserable animals. She retrieved her windbreaker and hoodie.

Seagn got down from the truck and unlocked the trailer. The animals were excited for food.

As she fed them, Seagn heard a woman call "Morning," from the entrance of the trailer. She turned to see Steph standing there with an umbrella and a long coat.

"Hey," Seagn said, walking through the trailer to her. Rain misted in the trailer, getting everything wet.

"Looks like a shitty day," she said. "You don't have a tent up for the animals."

"There's no space, and nothing to tie the tent down with. I only have one tent and two spots."

"Should have thought of that before you set up two spots. Don't expect any money for today." She walked away.

Maisey came out of the pig pen and flipped her tail up at Steph when she walked away. "Yeah," said Seagn. "That's how I feel."

Maisey and Seagn found a relatively dry spot in the hay. Maisey cuddled with Seagn, purring and rubbing her face into Seagn's hand.

Moose came over, wearing a cotton hoodie in the rain. "They're probably gonna call it," he said, climbing into the trailer. "Forecast sucks."

"What happens when they do that?"

"We sit around and do nothing and don't get paid."

"For the whole weekend?"

"What's the weather say for tomorrow?"

She checked her phone. Moose reached out and Maisey purred under his touch. Moose smiled at the cat.

"The weather tomorrow is in the sixties with clouds, but no rain."

Suddenly, Seagn heard bells, like someone ringing a Christmas bell from the Salvation Army. Moose got up. "Meeting," he said. "C'mon."

She got down, locking the trailer, and followed Moose to the RV. She saw Steph ringing a bell three times, then pausing, then again. People from the carnival gathered in the rain beyond the awning that covered the front of the RV.

"Come back at noon," said Webby. "No pay 'til then."

People walked away, grumbling. Beyond the RV, Seagn saw the parking lot was full of cars. Obviously, the rain didn't stop the store from opening.

Moose said, "Why don't we check out the trucks over at that used car lot?"

Seagn shrugged. "Might as well."

They walked in the rain down the hill, across the street and next to the Applebee's. No one was in the lobby when they walked in, taking down their hoods.

"Hello!" said a bald man coming out from behind a wall. "Crappy day for sales today, huh?"

"We're looking for a little pickup," said Moose.

The man nodded to Seagn. "For you, I take it."

"Yes," Seagn said.

"I'm David, co-owner." David held out his hand, and the two of them shook. "First off, what's your budget?"

"Eight grand."

David bit his bottom lip, looking out the windows of the lobby. "We have a couple. Can you drive a stick?"

"Yes."

"Does it need to be four-wheel drive?"

"No."

"Good, because that's at least ten. I got a Chevy Canyon out here … Let me get my coat."

He brought them to a forest green truck with a sticker on it. He held up the keys. "Take her for a spin?"

"How much?"

"The ride? Free."

"No, how much is the truck?"

"Eight five, but we can negotiate."

Seagn sighed. "I'm not in the mood to negotiate."

"Eight five with free registration."

Seagn reached for the keys. "I'll take it for a ride."

She peered inside. It was a stick shift. The inside was grayish-white, and she took a whiff of the air inside the vehicle — no smoke.

Moose climbed in beside her. "Roomy."

It had the normal controls for audio, hands-free calling, and Internet, something lacking from even the big truck. She started it up, and it sounded like it wasn't even running.

The VW was a stick, so she was used to driving with a clutch. It just took a few times to find where the clutch grabbed the gear on this one. It had five speeds and was a V6. The interior was skimpy, but the power behind the truck was impressive, especially when she took it out on the highway.

Moose looked like he loved it. Seagn was unimpressed. She just needed a workhorse, nothing with serious power. Even a four-cylinder would be fine for her. She wasn't looking for impressive.

"What do you think?" Moose asked as they started back to the dealer.

She shook her head.

Moose looked disappointed.

She pulled back into the car lot, and David came out to meet them.

"I want a four-cylinder," said Seagn, handing the keys back. "With a stick."

"You want a basic truck."

"Nothing special, really."

"There's this Taco. Those trucks you have to take a shotgun to them to kill 'em."

The Tacoma was silver, looked well-worn, and had 52,000 miles on it. It was also cheaper, coming in at seven-two. She took it for a ride and found it to be perfect for her needs. For seven-five, she had it registered.

Seagn watched the balance in her account dip even further down. Her last paycheck from the practice had come through, and the rent payment was due next week. She needed to buy more food for the animals.

At noon, she pulled into the area with the trucks. Joe stopped and patted the tailgate. "Nice!"

"Better be, for what I paid for it."

"Totally worth it," said Moose.

Seagn pocketed the keys and followed Joe to the RV and the ringing bell. Less people had returned than the morning.

As soon as they showed up, Webby said, "Come back at four."

Seagn threw her hands up. "Why don't you just —"

Moose elbowed her.

Webby gave her a glare before going back into the RV.

"Why doesn't he —"

"Because it admits to everyone not to bother coming back."

Seagn used her phone to find a place where she could buy farm feed and more hay. "There's a place north of here that sells farm stuff. Want to come for the ride?"

"Beats sitting here, smoking my pack," said Moose.

•   •   •

Seagn stared at her phone, at the balance on her bank account, while Moose unloaded the feed and two bales of hay into the trailer. She was burning through money like a drunken sailor. She had just under five thousand dollars left in her bank account.

"Where'd you get the money for that truck?" demanded Fatsy, as Moose hefted the last bale.

"Sugar Mommy," he said, nodding to Seagn.

Fatsy grinned. "Oh, is she?"

"She bought me dinner. What has she done for you lately?"

"You two —"

"No," snapped Seagn from the trailer.

Fatsy only laughed and walked away, waving his hand in dismissal. Seagn looked heavenward, and Moose only laughed.

"The rumors," said Seagn, looking back at her phone.

"So what?" Moose hefted the bale of hay into the trailer. "What do you care about Fatsy spreading rumors?" He brushed his gloved hands on his jeans. "There. All set."

"Thanks for your help."

"It's in exchange for dinner."

Seagn nodded.

"You're distracted."

"I'm running out of money fast."

"Don't worry. It'll turn a profit."

"I'm not worried about a profit. I'm worried that these guys won't survive the season and all this would have been for nothing."

Moose walked up to her. "Listen. You're doing better than Fatsy did. He'd dump something in the dumpster at least once a week."

Her mouth dropped open. "Are you serious?"

"Dead serious."

"My God."

"So just think, these guys are better off with you. I haven't seen a dead goat yet."

"Though Tommy isn't doing so great. He's eating, but he's still lethargic."

Moose tilted his head.

"Not active."

"Oh. Maybe he's tired."

"He's sick. I don't know what's wrong. I don't have the right tools to diagnose him. All I have is a stethoscope. I think it's an ulcer, or something in his stomach because he's tender there. I need an ultrasound — or an x-ray at the very least."

Moose glanced at the goat pen, where the five goats gathered miserably in the wet air. Thomas lay against the trailer grating, sleeping.

"You're a country vet now. You don't have all that."

Seagn frowned. "I know. I feel so helpless." She walked over to the goat pen. "I should take them for a walk or something. Give them air."

"There's plenty of air here. You're just bored."

"That's true."

Moose took out a cigarette. "Should take up smoking. Gives you something to do."

"No thanks."

He lit the cigarette with the lighter in his pocket. "Suit yourself."

At four, less people gathered in front of the RV. "We're going to open. There's some diehards who want rides; we'll give it to them."

A couple of the rides like the bouncy house and the carousel weren't open because of the rain, and neither were Seagn's animals. Seagn cleared away the wet hay from the two pens and put them in paper waste bags. According to the phone, the weather tomorrow was supposed to be much nicer. She would set up the pens again in the early morning.

In the meantime, she fed the animals, and went to sleep early.

•   •   •

The next morning dawned overcast, chilly in the wee hours, but it promised to be a good day without rain.

Seagn put clean, dry hay down in the two spots and herded the animals to their pens. They were ready by nine, when the carnival and the store opened.

They tried to make up for lost revenue. Tickets were two dollars instead of a dollar-fifty, with rides requiring two or three tickets each. The bouncy house and carousel were the only ones that used one ticket. The price of the food was jacked up from last weekend as well.

Meanwhile, Seagn watched the animals with people. They seemed tame enough: no biting by the animals. She'd have to have rules with them. No toddlers with the goats because they jumped on people. The sheep and ram continually butted into the fencing, so maybe no kids with them, either. The cow was too big. Shet would be slated for short horseback rides for little kids.

Little kids could touch the animals through the fence. And feed them from the paper bags that way, too.

The day went by fast, with Seagn constantly picking up the animals' messes. At six, the carnival closed, and began teardown early.

The animals trudged back to the trailer without giving her a hard time. She cleaned up the hay and fencing, and was done by midnight.

Seagn took a catnap for a couple of hours, knowing she'd have to drive the pickup in the convoy back to The Ranch. She'd probably need a Red Bull or some other energy drink to get her past sunrise.

Moose woke Seagn up. "Rise and shine. Ready to drive back?"

"Yeah." Seagn yawned and stretched.

"You're in the rear. Follow Maggie or you'll get lost."

The pickup didn't have satellite GPS, and she didn't know where The Ranch exactly was in Kittery, Maine, anyway. They drove the entire way straight without stopping.

7

S EAGN USED HER PHONE to look for farms in the area. Once she found a farm, she could get fresh hay and ask them if they can tell her where to get food.

Bakersfield Farm seemed the closest to her location, so she called them. Sure, they would sell her hay. For $50 a bale.

"No, thanks." Wrights sold it to her for $25 a bale, and the place in Worcester was $30. She made a few more calls before her phone went dead.

The cheapest was $20, at Bondgarden Farms only ten minutes away. If she caught them during harvest time, it was half the price. She took a walk over to Moose's truck.

"Him and Joe went to town," said Maggie, coming by.

"Oh. I guess I'll wait."

Maggie offered a cigarello. Seagn shook her head. When Maggie lit it up, it smelled like roses mixed with tobacco. A little overpowering, so Seagn moved out of the way of the smoke.

93

"So, what do you think?" Maggie asked after blowing smoke rings.

"About?"

"Your decision to buy the zoo."

She looked over at Thomas. He had gotten lethargic again, wasn't eating. "One of the goats is really sick. I don't know if it's contagious or if it's something he's got. I need an x-ray or an ultrasound. And even if it's an ulcer, I can't do much about it without the right drugs."

"You'd give drugs to a goat?"

"You'd give it to a person."

"Where do you get these drugs?"

"From a vet. I'm qualified to get them."

Maggie blew more rings. "Do you have any right now?"

"Sure."

"For pain?"

"I have some anesthesia, yes."

Maggie leaned in. "Can humans use it?"

"Yes, in the right doses."

"Really?" She looked thoughtful. "How do you do it? Like an IV or a pill?"

"Just a shot in the local area. It's a local anesthetic. But if I have to euthanize an animal, it's through an IV."

"How much does it take to kill an animal?"

"The stuff I have? Not much at all."

"Is it painless?"

"As painless as death can be, I would think. I don't know."

Maggie said nothing, just stared out into space.

"I'm going back to my trailer. Let Moose know I'm looking for him?"

"Yep, sure."

Seagn went back to the animals. She played with the goats and sheep while waiting for Moose.

When Moose arrived, he scowled at her.

"What? What did I do?"

"Did you tell Maggie you had drugs?"

"Yes—"

"Don't do that. Most of the people here are junkies and would steal them."

"But they're dangerous in the wrong dose."

"All the more reason people would steal them. I would keep them under lock and key if I were you."

"But they don't get a person high."

"They don't know that. All they know is that there's drugs. If it kills you, oh well." He still looked angrily at her. "Don't trust anyone around here."

"Except you?"

"That's up to you. You're new at this. I'm only trying to help."

Seagn glanced at the big truck, where she kept the black bag. She usually left it unlocked because she didn't have anything that anyone would want — until now.

"Maybe I should put it in the pickup."

"Someone will break into it."

"Carry it around?"

"Someone will attack you for it."

"Well, what?"

Moose turned to the truck. "Go get the drugs and bring them with us when we go to town."

"We're not going to town. We're going to a farm."

"Good. Because we're going to hide them in the truck without anyone but you and me knowing where it is."

"I thought you just said someone would break in."

"They will. You have insurance on it, right?"

"Of course."

"Hope you have glass coverage."

•   •   •

Seagn pulled into the main road leading to the farm. She had made an appointment before showing up with Moose.

A shepherd mix greeted them when they pulled in. "Hi, puppy," Seagn said, scratching the dog behind the ears. It made happy sounds, bumping up against Seagn's legs.

"Tilly, come here," called a man, and Seagn looked up to see a very good-looking man with brown hair under a baseball cap and dark eyes. "I'm Carl. We spoke on the phone?"

"Yeah. Shaun." They shook hands. "This is Moose. He's my assistant."

"Official schlepper, are you?" Carl shook hands with Moose.

Moose grunted. "Seems so."

Carl put his thumbs through the loops of his jeans and looked so much like a Midwestern farmer that it made Seagn smile. "So, what can I interest you in?"

"Do you have any animals?"

"Horses mostly."

"Where do you get the feed from?"

"Smith's Hill. They deliver."

"Do you have their contact information?"

"I'll get it for you. Hang out right here. Tilly, come on, hon."

The shepherd mix followed Carl into the house. Moose turned to the truck. "I think I found a place for your bag. Do you have anything in it that's harmless to people?"

"Saline? Salt water."

"Will it kill someone if they inject it?"

"No."

"Get some, put it under here with a syringe." He patted the driver's seat. "They'll break in and once they find it, they'll stop looking."

Then he went to the rear passenger's side. The rear cab was tiny, not really made for another person of full adult size. He pulled on the seat and it came out.

"Put the rest here." Moose pointed to the back of the seat.

"I'm going to have to take the seat out to get it?"

"The object of hiding something is to make sure it's somewhere people can't get at easily. You lock it up or you hide it. Or do both."

"That defeats the whole purpose of having an emergency bag. I can't get at it quickly."

"Fine, then they'll steal your shit."

The door opened and Carl stepped out to see the two of them glaring at each other. He looked from one to the other and said, "Um, excuse me?"

They both turned to Carl.

"Was I interrupting?"

"A discussion," said Seagn, walking toward Carl.

"An argument, more like." Carl smiled, handed out a card to Seagn. "Here's where they're located. About twenty miles up the road from here if you want to go see."

Moose shoved the black bag in the upper part of the rear seat and forced the seat back into place. It didn't look like it had been taken out. But it wasn't easy to get at.

"How many bales of hay do you need?"

"Four."

"I'll give you five for the price of four."

Seagn held up her phone. "You take phones?"

"Who doesn't?"

Everyone living at The Ranch, she thought.

Carl held up his phone. Seagn opened her bank app and transferred $80 to his bank.

"Pull right into the barn."

Carl used a pulley to drop four bales into the pickup, which filled it up pretty quickly. Seagn and Moose tied down the fifth bale so it wouldn't slide across the four bales that took up the bed.

"Pleasure doing business," said Carl.

"I'll be coming here often between gigs."

"A traveling petting zoo, huh? Make any money with it?"

"Not yet. I'm going to offer bags of feed for sale and have kids hand-feed them."

"You know what I saw in a zoo? A bubble gum machine with pellets in it."

It went against Seagn's nature to use pellets. She preferred a more organic feed because the nutrients were cooked out of the pellets. But if they were given as treats, maybe it wouldn't be too bad. Once in a while.

"Let me think about it."

"Otherwise you have to dispose of the bags, because people are stupid and will throw them on the ground and your animals might eat them."

"I'll put a wastepaper basket near the entrance or something."

"Good luck with that. I hope to see you again soon."

Seagn got in the truck. Moose climbed in and yanked hard on the seatbelt when he got in. She used her phone's GPS to find Smith's, saw that it was listed as a "country store".

"I'm going to get some feed, okay?"

He shrugged, not looking at her.

"Are you still mad at me because of what I said?"

"No," he said, and turned his head to look out the side window.

"You're mad at me."

"I'm not mad at you. I will be if you keep pushing it."

Seagn shoved the truck into drive and peeled out of the dirt driveway.

They drove for maybe five minutes before she said, "You know, maybe you're right."

"About?"

"Someone breaking in to steal the drugs. It's not that uncommon for vets to end up using their own drugs."

Moose let out a breath. "I'm not mad at that."

"You *are* mad."

He shook his head, turned to look at her when they stopped at a light. "It's not mad, it's … weird. Never mind, okay? It's fine. I'm okay. See?" He smiled at her.

A person behind them beeped, making her start the truck moving again.

"Someone's in a hurry," Moose said.

"Big hurry." The person passed them, flipping them the bird as he did.

"Fuck him," Moose said. "Watch him get into an accident."

"If I got bent out of shape every time someone passed me, I'd be a wreck."

"No road rage?"

"Road irritation, not rage."

Smith's Hill was a large sprawling store with everything from eggs and milk to two-by-fours and bags of cement. They didn't seem to carry health and beauty aids, though. It was a man's store.

Seagn smelled fresh cedar wood when she walked in. The store had exposed beams and rough-hewn wooden shelves with some toys, candy, and other kid-friendly things at their level. Stacked above them were tools, light bulbs, and lanterns. Ropes and cables of all types hung from the ceiling. Copper pots and pans hung in another section, along with cast-iron ones stacked beneath them.

Seagn loved the smell, inhaling deeply. A woman was at the counter with an old-fashioned cash register with huge buttons on them. "Can I help you?"

"I'm looking for animal feed for goats and sheep, pigs, a cow, and a horse."

"The whole farm, huh?" The woman chuckled, pulled out a tablet.

"No chickens. Organic food, please."

Through a mirror on the other side of the room, she saw Moose's eyes roll.

"And treats."

"Sure, we have some in stock. Might have to special order for the pigs because most people around here give them slop."

"I can't. It's a petting zoo and it wouldn't look good to have people watching pigs eat chicken bones."

"People petting pigs?"

"City people. Tourists."

"Strange," the woman said, shaking her head. "All right —" she showed Seagn the tablet.

Seagn read through the details for each of the bags of feed, made her selections, and special ordered organic food for the pigs, even though they ate almost anything. They could eat the goat/sheep food for now.

"Do you have small bags for sale?"

"Three-by-four?" The woman held up a plastic bag used for the bulk candy.

"Got any paper bags? I'd like to be as organic as possible."

Seagn saw Moose look heavenward.

"Just these plastic bags."

"I'll take a few hundred of them, then."

After Seagn paid with her phone, the woman said, "Go round back and we'll load it up."

Moose moved out of Seagn's way as he turned around sharply to go back to the truck.

"Organic? Really?"

"I'm producing methane gas, so I might as well try to tamp down waste."

"Bella is producing methane gas."

"All of them are."

"I haven't heard the goats fart."

Seagn climbed into the cab of the truck and said, "You'll know it when they do."

•　　•　　•

Moose finished unloading the bales using a rusty dolly Seagn had found in the back of the trailer. "You need a new dolly," Moose said, dragging it up the ramp, its wheels not moving.

"You know how much those go for?"

"I do. Costco had them for $50."

"I'm not driving all the way back to Worcester to save a couple of bucks on a dolly."

"Should have gotten it at Smith's. They had one there for $89.99. Probably organic, too."

"Will you stop with the organic stuff?" She put her hand on her hip.

He laughed. "You started it with the organic paper bags."

"Don't you feel guilty leaving behind non-organic items?"

"Nope. Because I won't be around long enough to care."

"If I can, I will." She held up the plastic bags. "Let's fill these with a half a cup or so of the pellets."

"About how much is that?"

She looked at his large hands. "Half a handful?"

She lined them up as he filled them and zipped them closed at the top.

As they were working, someone came over — a dark Hispanic man they hadn't seen before with a thick mustache and beady dark eyes.

"Hey, they say you a doctor?"

"I'm a veterinarian. An animal doctor."

"Animal doctor?"

"Yes. I don't know anything about humans. Why?"

"*Mi amigo*. In pain."

"She doesn't have any of that shit, Hugo," said Moose.

"Heroin?" His eyes lit up when he said the word.

She shook her head. "No heroin."

"*Mi perro*. In pain."

"You don't have a fucking dog," said Moose. "Get the fuck outta here."

Hugo looked dejected. Seagn watched Moose, who was giving him an evil eye and flaunting that "Don't Fuck With Me" aura that Joe had mentioned. Hugo turned away, his head bowed, shuffling back to the trucks. Some people must have joined the crew at The Ranch since last week, and the rumor of drugs had gone around already.

"Be careful," said Moose. "They're watching you."

•   •   •

"If you think about it," said Seagn, as she sipped on the red wine she had brought to the fire and only she was drinking, "even if I did have drugs, they wouldn't be powerful enough for a human to get anything out of them."

The small group had gathered together at the firepit again that night. Moose suggested she put the rumor to bed or she would be constantly looking over her shoulder.

Maggie started, "But you said —"

"I said I have access. I didn't say I *had* them."

Said Joe, "How do you get access?"

"I have to go to a vet's practice and apply. Then it'll take six months or so before they trust me with prescriptions."

The lies came easily, being that there was some truth in them. Moose coached her, letting her weave the tale of how difficult it was to get euthanasia drugs.

Hugo and his friend sat near the fire. A reed-thin man who chain-smoked examined everyone one at a time, assessing them.

"Six months?" asked Maggie.

"In the same practice, yes."

"You don't have any drugs on you now?"

"Nope." She sipped her wine.

"Oh." Everyone looked down. Seagn glanced at Moose who barely nodded his head once. Carlos got up first, then Hugo and his friend, dragging themselves herself away. Seagn took a deep breath and set her wine glass down on the ground.

"Where's the next stop this weekend?"

"Stoughton," said Joe. "Half of us there; half of us at Milford."

"Where am I going?"

"Hell if I know. Ask Webby."

She glanced at the RV to see that the light was still on inside. It was only eight at night, so she didn't think she'd interrupt him if she went now. She got up, but Moose shook his head.

"Wait until the morning."

"He's up."

"He's probably watching baseball. You don't want to interrupt him when he's watching baseball."

Seagn plopped herself down on the grass. "I can't believe how you all kowtow to him."

"He pays us," said Joe. "You might be rich, but not all of us are."

Seagn looked at her wine glass, thinking about those words. Compared to the people there, she *was* rich. She finished drinking the wine, gathered her bottle and blanket, and left.

"Shaun," called Moose, running to catch up to her.

"I'm never going to fit in," she said. "You all bow to Webby. You all think I'm rich."

"It's not like you're doing anything to fit in," said Moose quietly.

"What?"

"Wine. In a glass."

"What's wrong with that?"

"We share it out of the bottle. You've seen it."

"But since the Pandemic —"

"It's been over for five years."

Seagn put a hand on her hip. She didn't see Moose's reaction. "I'm a doctor. I'm cognizant of germs."

"And you talk rich."

Seagn almost snarled the next two words. "Excuse me."

"Yes, ma'am."

She turned and went back to her trailer. She gathered Maisey and brought her to the front of the truck. The rest of the animals kept quiet through the night.

•   •   •

The next morning, she stood in the dawn outside of Webby's RV.

"Where am I going tomorrow?"

"Can I have a cup of coffee before I answer you?" Webby asked, as he stepped outside of the RV to the table set up under the awning.

"No."

"Steph!"

"What?"

"Where's the petting zoo going?"

"Stoughton. Leaving tomorrow."

"Milford's leaving this afternoon," Webby said. "Be ready to leave in the morning."

Seagn went back to the trailer to straighten up so that the animals would be comfortable on new hay. In the afternoon, she watched as some of the trucks and the RV left. Later on, when she looked back at what was left, she noticed that Moose's truck was gone.

She didn't panic, not until sunset when Moose didn't return. The RV left as well. The few items remaining were two food trucks, the bouncy house, and the Tilt-A-Whirl. Only the petting zoo and Tilt-A-Whirl were semi-trucks.

Seagn packed the animals away and stayed up all night, wondering how she was going to get down to Stoughton. She didn't have anyone's phone number, so it wasn't like she could call to get someone to drive her down. She didn't have the proper license to drive the semi-truck. And besides, she didn't know how to drive such a large vehicle.

The next morning the rest of the convoy started up, and Seagn stood stupidly at her trailer.

"You going?" Hugo called from the passenger side of the Tilt-A-Whirl.

"I don't know how to drive this truck."

Hugo turned to the driver and said something, then Hugo turned back to Seagn. He gave her a shrug at the same time the Tilt-A-Whirl driver, Hugo's friend, jumped down from his cab.

"What you mean you can't drive? You got a truck, don't you?"

"This is a semi. I don't know how to drive it."

"It's just bigger. Follow me. Do what I do."

Seagn gaped open-mouthed at the driver's back as he walked to the truck. She got into the cab on the driver's side and stared at the dashboard that looked all the world like one for an airplane. She started the beast, and it rumbled under her.

The steering wheel was huge as she turned it, so the truck took a very wide right-hand turn. She fumbled getting it on the wide path, directly behind the Tilt-A-Whirl. At least there wasn't a clutch, but still she crawled behind the other truck, her knuckles white as she held onto the steering wheel.

She had to take a left-hand turn, which she did widely again, following the other driver. It took a short drive on Route 1, then onto I-95.

The traffic wasn't bad on this Friday morning. She was terrified, though, as she watched the speedometer creep up from 25 to 60. *As long as I stay behind the truck, I should be all right.*

Please, God.

8

S EAGN VOWED, AS SHE PUT THE TRUCK IN PARK, the cold
sweat of fear dripping off her, to never, ever, *ever*, do this
again without having someone teach her how to drive a big rig.
She almost clipped two cars taking turns, and barely got the
trailer onto the field in one piece.

She got out of the cab, shaking and sweating, and leaned
against the closed door, taking big gulps of air.

The three other trucks started setting up as soon as they got
to the spot. Seagn needed time to get her nerves to stop jangling.
She held out her hand and saw that it was shaking.

She slid down the truck to her knees and came close to
bawling. Hugo noticed and said something to his friend who was
putting up the fencing for the Tilt-A-Whirl. They came running
over to her. By then, she was on all fours, throwing up.

"*Mira, mira,*" said Hugo over and over.

"Hey, hey, lady."

Seagn took a breath and sat back.

"You okay now?"

Seagn nodded, her eyes closed, not saying anything.

"We'll help you as soon as we're done, okay? Just rest here, okay?"

Again, she nodded, and tried not to look at her puke on the manicured grass.

The men put up the fencing by the time she was able to stand. They were fast and efficient.

The woman from the fried dough truck came to her. "Hi." She offered Seagn a bottled water. "Two dollars."

Seagn fumbled in her pocket for the money, thinking at first that she was kidding. She wasn't. She handed over the two dollars.

"You gonna be okay? You're not prego, are you?"

"Prego? No, of course not."

"Then why you pukin'?"

"Nerves."

The woman snorted. "Nerves." She turned around to see Hugo and the driver coming her way. "Whatevs. See ya."

Seagn took a swig of the water and spit it out to get the bad taste out of her mouth.

Hugo asked for the keys to the trailer to open the back. They found the tent and set that up, then strung up the lights. By then, Seagn was feeling better and set up the fencing while they did the lights.

"We not on until tomorrow," said Hugo's friend, eyeing her as if she had something he wanted.

"I can't drive the truck back."

He looked at her, then the truck. "*Si.*"

"Does Webby have a phone?"

The driver shrugged.

Seagn glanced at the truck the rides came on, searching for a phone number. It only read "Rockwell Amusements".

Her phone was down to 20%, but she used it to get the phone number. When she called it, Steph's voice came on saying no one was available, but if she'd like to leave a mess —

Disgusted, she hung up. Using the USB connector inside the truck, she connected the charger for the phone.

She didn't have to put down hay. She went into the trailer and played with the goats until sunset.

There was a Subway within walking distance, so she got her dinner there. She also got a small cup of "tuna" for Maisey, who had brought no mice to her in the last few days. After locking up the door, she went to bed and slept like a log.

At sunrise, she brought the animals out. Tommy was sick again, not eating, so she left him behind in the trailer. People were up in the morning walking their dogs and came by the Commons to see what was going on. One small Yorkie was excited by the goats, who fed off his excitement, and bounced along the edge of the fencing to see them. Seagn smiled at the dog's owner, a man in a Patriots hoodie who smiled back.

"Your dog likes them," Seagn said.

"Can I touch them?"

"That's what they're there for."

The man reached out and pet Mohawk's small horns. "It's a petting zoo?"

"Yep. I'll have some feed out for kids to feed them if they want."

"I'll bring my daughter. She'd love that."

"That'll be great." She held out her hand. "Shaun."

"Paul. This is Mac."

The Yorkie licked her hand and nuzzled against her leg. "Hello, Mac. I don't have any cookies for you. Unless you want some horse feed."

Paul laughed. "I don't think he'd care much for that. He's a finicky eater." He glanced at Bella, the cow. "How long are you here until?"

"Sunday night, maybe? I know we tear down on Sunday, but no one's told me the time."

"We'll be around later. Nice to meet you."

"Nice meeting you too. I hope to see your daughter."

Paul waved, tugged Mac away from the animals, and headed back down the street. Seagn went back to the trailer and sat on the edge, her feet dangling, waiting for the animals to do their business so she could clean them up.

About an hour later, another man came to the animals. This man was in a suit and tie and had a disgusted look on his face.

"Hey!" he yelled at the sheep. "Don't eat the grass."

"It's what sheep do," said Seagn.

"This is special grass."

Seagn raised her eyebrows. "Special grass?"

"It takes a lot of work to keep this grass up. Now they'll eat it down to the soil. And are you cleaning up after them? Animal feces and urine will discolor the grass."

Seagn put a hand on her hip. "Yes, I'm cleaning up after them."

"Who's the owner? We never agreed to farm animals being put here."

"I'm the owner of these animals, and I was told to be here by Web— Mr. Webster."

"Now the goats are eating the grass! And that cow is eating the grass, too!"

"Animals do that," said Seagn. "Who are you, exactly?"

"I'm on the town council, and we didn't approve anything for animals."

"Well, take it up with Mr. Webster, Mister …?"

"DeCosta. And you bet I will! Stop them from eating the grass."

"Sure," Seagn said.

The man turned and went to the other ride and started yelling something at Hugo.

Seagn rolled her eyes and turned to the goats. "Enjoy the grass."

•　　•　　•

They opened officially at nine a.m. Amazingly enough, people lined up for the fried dough by ten. There was enough room on the field for the entire Rockwell Amusements set-up. But surrounding the rides were vendors and artists arrayed with small canopy tents and tables. Behind Seagn was an oil painter who had the ugliest, darkest paintings she'd ever seen. Next to her was a beader — a very talkative woman who never gave her name but fed bread to Bella and half an apple to Shet.

Seagn made small bags of food for each of the animals, selling them first for fifty cents. Then she realized people would pay a dollar for one because no one could dig out the change.

Bella and the goats were a hit. Kids fed them and laughed and pet the animals. The parents were leery of the pigs — they weren't covered in dirt or anything. They were just pigs. The sheep were jealous and bleated often.

At one point, a toddler got into the goat pen, no parents in sight. Of course, two goats were excited to see someone with a bag, and they jumped, knocking the toddler to the ground and making him cry.

Now the parent appeared, a heavy woman bowling her way through into the pen. The goats, not knowing any better, aimed for the bag that the toddler held tightly. The mother picked up the toddler and looked around yelling, "Who owns this?"

Seagn sighed inwardly and stepped forward.

"Your animals are unruly!" The woman bounced the child to try and get him to stop crying. It wasn't working. "You should take better care of them."

Before Seagn could say anything else, the woman shoved by her.

"Sorry," Seagn called after her. Not that she meant it.

She would have to hang a sign that read "Ages 6 and up" or something like that. She was more careful handing out the bags of treats.

Paul arrived when she was down to her last three bags. He came alone.

"Where's your daughter?"

He hunched his shoulders. "Her Mom took her this weekend."

"Oh." She handed a bag of treats to him. "I saved this for her. Do you want to feed any of the animals?"

His eyes lit up. "I'd love to, thanks."

He didn't bother with the goats. They had their fans. Instead, he walked over to the sheep who pushed each other aside to get closer to the fence. Bob, the ram, snorted and gave him a look of contempt, as if groveling for food was beneath him.

"They're so soft," said Paul, petting the sheep.

"They've just been sheared."

Paul scratched Dorothy's side, his fingers digging into the sheep's skin. He finished giving them the food and got up from his crouching position. "Will you be here tomorrow?"

"Until we close, yes."

"With more food?"

"If you want, you can stick around until I feed them tonight. After closing time."

"I'd like that."

The crowd thinned out to curious onlookers and kids who could get their hands through the fencing to pet the animals. She expected the woman with the crying toddler to show up with the police or the SPCA. She never did.

At eleven, the lights started to go out along the carnival, and Seagn kept hers on so she could have light to herd the animals by. Webby wasn't around screaming at her to shut the lights off.

Paul arrived as she unlatched one of the fences for the goats. "They know where to go in the trailer," Seagn said. "Can you just follow them and make sure they go there?"

"Sure."

Paul was a little too overprotective. The second a goat stepped off the trajectory, he was there to make sure the goat stayed on the path to the trailer. Seagn brought the pigs one at a time, then the sheep and ram. Last, she brought the horse and Paul the cow.

"I think there's a dead goat in your trailer."

"Oh, no …"

Seagn ran into the trailer. Tommy didn't even raise his head. In the dim light she saw his labored breathing, the rise and fall of his side. She felt helpless without her medicine bag — why did she have to listen to Moose and lock it up? Now it was miles away and this goat was suffering.

"Is there an emergency vet around here?" she asked Paul.

"About an hour away."

She looked to Paul, then the goat, then back to Paul.

"Is it bad?" Paul asked.

"It's very bad. I'm a vet. I don't have my bag with me, but he's got fluid in his lungs. I can hear it when he's breathing."

"I'll give you a ride there."

She carried Tommy, a good hundred pounds of dead weight, to the front of the trailer. Paul took him from her arms while she locked the door.

"Car's this way," he said, and brought her out onto the empty street. A block down, he said, "Left coat pocket has the keys."

Seagn fished them out and pressed the remote. A dark car beeped and flashed a few yards in front of them. It was an Audi, royal blue, almost black, with a spacious back seat. Luckily, it was covered with a blanket, probably for the dog.

Paul gently placed Tommy across the back seat. Then they drove the forty-five minutes to the emergency vet.

• • •

"I'm sorry," Seagn said for probably the thirtieth time that night while they drove back to the gig.

Paul gave her a tired smile. "It's all right, really."

"You probably had plans."

"I did, but it all worked out."

Seagn looked out the window. "I'm sorry, I'm just not in the mood for —"

"I get it. I'm not asking for that right now."

"Believe me, I think I need something like that right now." Seagn sighed.

"I can stay with you until dawn. Then I really need to get some sleep."

"No," Seagn said. "Just bring me back to the zoo and you go to bed."

"I'll come by later, if that's okay."

Seagn smiled, also worn out. "That'll be nice, thank you." She studied him. "If you don't mind my asking, why did you get a divorce?"

"Honestly? I'm too nice." He chuckled along with Seagn. "That's what she told me. I wasn't a good disciplinarian to Sarah, our daughter. Then she cheated on me, so I let it go on for a good long while."

"Did you love your wife?"

"I did." He shrugged. "Maybe I still do sometimes. Mac is always there to take care of, and he gives unconditional love."

"Pets are great," Seagn said.

"You have different pets."

"Exotic to people who don't live near a farm."

"I sometimes wish I could be a vet. But then I'd have days like today …"

Again, a sigh from Seagn. "Yeah, that doesn't help. But I'm alleviating their suffering is what I tell myself."

"It's a calling."

"It really is."

They fell silent for the last few miles.

Paul dropped her off at the edge of the carnival. Her lights were still on, but the animals were asleep with the noisy generator going. She shut it off and the silence of the area washed over her for a short time. Some pre-dawn birds tweeted to greet the morning.

I would sleep with him, but I can't. I'm in mourning.

She dragged herself into the truck, setting her phone alarm for ten, as they weren't open until noon on Sunday. That would give her six hours of sleep and hopefully time to set up the animals before opening.

After what seemed a short nap, someone banged on the truck's door. She rolled over to see the sunlight peeking between the shades on the windshield. Her phone said it was 6:34 in the morning.

The banging continued. "Shaun? It's Moose."

Seagn stumbled out of the rear cot and opened the door.

Moose grinned. "Hey! I heard you had a panic attack driving the truck. So I'm here!"

Seagn watched his grin dissipate at the look on her face. "Bad time?"

"I just got to bed."

"How come?"

"Tommy died."

Moose tilted his head.

"The sick goat I inherited from Fatsy."

"You got four other goats."

"He didn't have to be sick."

"Are we going to talk about what an asshole Fatsy is? Because I saw this movie before."

"Nevermind." Seagn slammed the door on him.

She heard Moose talking to himself, then the roar of the bike. She rolled back into her bed, but couldn't sleep. Was he not understanding like Paul? Paul understood what happened and empathized with her. Moose … was he just like Fatsy?

It was Moose's fault that she had to bring Tommy to the vet and face the inexpressive looks of the techs and veterinarian there. It was his fault she had to explain that the animal was sick when she got it, and she couldn't do anything about it. If she had her medicine bag, she could have alleviated Tommy's suffering and brought him to the vet for cremation without any explanation. But she had to listen to Moose talk about how everyone was a junkie or a thief.

She got out of bed. She needed a stiff black tea, or probably even an espresso. She changed her clothes, noting that she needed to do laundry this week. Seagn climbed out of the truck, yawning and stretching.

The coffee shop that had been open at dawn yesterday was closed today, and she didn't see another restaurant in the area. Just her luck.

The animals needed to get fed since she had neglected them the night before. They were probably angry at her now. She walked along the trailer and heard the sheep bleating.

"Yeah, I know. Bad owner. No biscuit." She unlocked the trailer, and the animals woke up, making noise.

She was feeding them in the trailer when she heard the motorcycle come back. Moose parked behind the truck and approached the trailer. "I got you an Egg McMuffin."

She nodded. "Sorry I was so short with you."

"Hey, I woke you up. I'm cranky when I get up, too." He thrust the bag at her.

She washed her hands with an alcohol wipe and settled down to eat. "How did you know I had a panic attack?"

"Diego called Webby."

"Who's Diego?"

"The guy with Hugo."

"He said he didn't have the phone number!"

"It's only used for emergencies."

Seagn exhaled sharply. "Do *you* have the phone number?"

"No. I'm not that special. Besides, this only happens once or twice a year, that we get separated."

"Hey, Shaun."

She looked up to see Paul with the Yorkie, Mac.

"Hey, Paul! This is Moose. He drives the truck."

Paul held out his hand "Nice to meet you."

Moose, his face clouded over in anger, shook Paul's hand. *Probably very hard*, Seagn thought.

Paul took his hand back gingerly. Seagn could sense the tension immediately after that. She could almost see the "Don't Fuck With Me" aura that Joe talked about, a red pulsing aura that surrounded Moose.

"I see you're busy," said Paul. "We just stopped by to say hello."

"Did you get any sleep?"

Moose whipped his head around to Seagn.

"A little. Then this guy saw the sunrise and had to go out." He smiled a little, tugged on the leash. "I'll catch up on it later. See you around. Nice —"

Moose glared knives at Paul.

"Right. Nice meeting you."

Moose grunted. When Paul retreated, his tail between his legs, Seagn hit Moose on the shoulder. "What did you do that for?"

"Do what?"

"You scared him."

"Not my fault he's a pussy. What do you mean did you sleep last night?"

"He brought me to the vet's when Tommy died. We didn't get back until about four."

"That's it?"

"What do you mean?" She turned to look steadily at Moose, who had bowed his head so that his long hair covered his face. "Do you think I slept with him?"

Seagn thought she could see red creeping up into his cheeks. "I didn't, okay?"

"Okay," he said, still looking down.

She wasn't sure what to feel. *Insulted? Warm and fuzzy that he cared?* She ate her food, trying not to smile. The predominant feeling was warm and fuzzy.

They ate in silence while the animals moved around in the trailer. One of the animals kicked at the mesh walls.

"I'd better check that," Seagn said.

"Yup."

She got up, finishing her sandwich as she walked to the back. Shet banged on the latch with his rear hooves, trying to kick it open. Bella mooed loudly.

"What? What?" She opened the pen and Shet came up to her. "What's wrong?"

Something black streaked between Shet's feet and the hay seemed to explode just beyond Shet's rear legs. Maisey rose out of the hay with a mouse in her mouth. She triumphantly carried the fresh carcass to Seagn.

"Scared of a little mouse? Look at the brave kitty who killed it for you." She chuckled, picked up the mouse by the tail and dropped it in the same plastic bag that she kept for the animals' litter.

Seagn pet Maisey and guided Shet out of the pen. Might as well start setting up.

•   •   •

"Your animals ate the grass," said DeCosta as she was setting up.

"I told them not to," Seagn stated. "They don't listen well, I guess."

"And they peed on it."

"They do that sometimes."

"That burns the grass! This is special Japanese grass! Kids run through it. People picnic on it. And your animals use it like the inside of a barn."

"They're farm animals, sir."

Moose tossed a cigarette butt on the grass and stomped it out. "PICK THAT UP!"

DeCosta's face was red. The vein in the middle of his forehead throbbed a prominent green. Seagn sighed, while Moose bent and picked it up. He put it in the garbage can Seagn had next to her. Seagn thought she could see him grinning under the long hair.

"Can't you put that somewhere else? It stinks."

"Not if I want access to it. Would you rather I leave their crap on your grass?"

She waited to see if he would blow up. Instead. he stomped away, his head swiveling this way and that, looking for someone.

"Is Webby around?" asked Seagn.

"Nope. He's back at The Ranch."

"He's looking for who's in charge of us."

"Don't look at me."

"You have the magic phone number."

"No, Diego does." Moose lit another cigarette. "Webby didn't want to be liable for any accidents. You're a terrible driver, according to Diego."

"That's because it's a semi. I can drive trucks."

"Speaking of which —."

"Oh, yeah, speaking of —"

"No one's broken into it yet."

"I'm taking out the medicine bag," Seagn said at the same time.

Moose tilted his head. "But someone —"

"If they overdose on rabies vaccine, that's their problem. Aren't we all adults here? I could have helped Tommy."

"They're not all adults," said Moose. "Suit yourself. Was only trying to help."

Mr. DeCosta returned at noon, a man with a disgusted look following behind him. Seagn was cleaning a stinking pile from Bella when he arrived.

"See? They use this area like it's a bathroom."

Seagn looked up from her work. "Hello," she said.

"Will that damage the grass?" asked the man with DeCosta.

"It'll probably fertilize it," Seagn said.

DaCosta nearly screamed, "That's disgusting! It doesn't fertilize the grass! Kids play on this grass!"

The other man turned to Seagn. "You must remove these animals immediately."

"If you don't mind my asking, but who are you?"

"The Committee Chairman."

Just then, one of the sheep let drop a pile. She *baa*'ed loudly to make sure everyone noticed.

Seagn shrugged. "Fine with me. But can I ask how I'm going to leave with all those tents surrounding my truck?"

She pointed to the vendor tents now set up near her trailer.

"Unless you want the animals in the trailer and have them stink up the area there. And excuse me while I pick up Rose's droppings."

She closed Bella's fencing, and then walked over to the sheep's pen, dragging her ever-present garbage can, dustpan, and broom.

The chairman looked from the vendors to the trailer, back to the animals.

"We close at five," said the chairman. "I suppose we can tolerate this for another four hours."

"It will cause damage!"

The chairman said, "She's cleaning up as best as she can. Unless she puts diapers on these animals, there's nothing we can do."

"But, Lev—"

"Sorry, Tony. We can't have these animals near the vendors. It's only four more hours. She was here all day yesterday, and I didn't hear one complaint."

"But the grass!"

The chairman put his arm around DeCosta's shoulders. "We'll fix it. Come on."

For four hours, Seagn diligently watched the animals, cleaning up after them. Moose took down the lights and the tent at 4:30 and, by 5:00, they were packing the animals in. Most of the vendors had packed up as well. An hour after closing, everything was set to go.

9

S EAGN DIDN'T REALIZE until she had finished feeding the animals that she had been involved with them for a month. The animals were much healthier now than they had been when she had bought them.

It rained on the Monday after they got back, so she kept the animals in the leaky trailer. It was a miserable couple of days — rainy, then overcast.

She moved her medicine bag to the big truck, tucking it under her bed and locking the door. She gathered her clothes, sheets, and blanket, and drove into Kittery looking for a laundromat. After twenty minutes of driving, she found one on Route 1 that advertised free dryers. Of course, that meant the washers were high-priced.

Seagn watched CNN while taking care of her clothes. Nothing important seemed to be going on. In a month, she hadn't missed a school shooting, a massacre, or a hundred-car pileup somewhere. No new wars, no new illnesses, no tornadoes, or major climate change storms heading through. A quiet month.

She also tried to figure out when would be a good time to get new animals. Chickens were out. So were ducks. Maybe geese. More goats and sheep. No more pigs, unless they were the little ones. Maybe she should stop by Bondgarden Farms to see if they had any animals for sale, or they could tell her where to get Shet some new shoes.

How was she going to transport him? Tie him down in the pickup truck? She'd have to rent a horse trailer. She wondered if the farm had that option available. She glanced at her dwindling savings and shook her head. Even with the cash in her pocket from Webby, she questioned whether she had enough to rent a trailer and get Shet's shoes.

Ping! Her email chime went off, and she read the note from her brother. She got to a part that made her gasp.

I'll be coming up to Salem after I graduate, and stay with you until my grad semester starts …

She hit the reply button. *I'm not in Salem. I'm on the road for the summer. I'm traveling with the petting zoo and the carnival I think I told you about.* So much had happened, she didn't remember if she told him or not. *Call me when you get a chance if you want.*

Seagn sent it off, and stared at the phone, willing Liam to call her. She looked over to see her dryer finished, so claimed her clothes.

As she folded her clothes, the phone chirped. It was a text message from Liam.

Can't call. You're doing what?

Traveling with a carnival. I bought their petting zoo side show.

Sick! Can I come?

No.

Where's the carnival going?

All over New England.

Why can't I come?

He was not built for working outside. She thought of her brother, overweight with his polos and khakis, hardly in a t-shirt, and never, ever, shirtless.

It's really hard work. Outside in the rain. During thunderstorms.

Seagn put the phone down and gathered her clothes. After she placed the phone on top of the pile, it chirped again. She stuffed her clothes in the trash bag she had brought them in and retrieved her phone.

Nevermind.

She smiled. "I thought you'd say that," she said to the phone, but texted, *Talk to you later.*

•　　•　　•

Seagn pulled into the farm and got out of the truck. Tilly greeted her again. "Hey, puppy, where's your pa?"

Tilly didn't seem to care where his owner was, as she was happy enough to roll on the ground in front of Seagn, exposing her belly for her to scratch. Seagn finally stopped, and the dog got up, butting her hand with her head.

Seagn walked around the barn, calling, "Carl? Hey? Anyone?"

"Yeah!" a man yelled back, deep within the barn. "Yeah, who's there?"

She walked into the barn and looked up toward where the voice was coming from. "Shaun. Is that you, Carl?"

"No." She looked up again into the loft to see a man standing at the edge of it, as if he was going to leap down the hundred or so feet to land on the ground. He had blond hair and was built solidly, a bull on legs.

"I'm Johnny. I work with Carl. What can I do for you?"

"Do you have any animals for sale?"

"Horses. Nothing else much, why?" He approached the ladder and swung around it, climbing down from the loft.

"Geese? Ducks?"

"No, no birds."

Seagn frowned. "Okay, next question. Where is your blacksmith?"

"You mean for horseshoes?"

"Yes."

"What kind of horse?"

"Shetland pony."

He jumped the short distance down two rungs to the ground. "Is he broken in?"

"Um …"

"What kind of work does he do?"

"He stands around in a petting zoo."

Johnny waved a hand. "He don't need shoes. Just trimming, that's all."

"He's got shoes on him. They're broken."

"We can take the shoes off him. You just need to trim him every eight to ten weeks or so."

"Then I need to get him trimmed and the shoes off. Do you know where I can go?"

"Bring him here?"

"Thought you'd say that. I need a trailer." She pointed out of the barn. "All I have is a truck."

Johnny frowned with one side of his mouth. "I'll meet you at your truck. Give me a few minutes."

She walked one way; he went the other. After ten minutes or so, she wasn't surprised to see him come back to the truck, a knapsack over his shoulder.

"If the horse can't come to me, I'll go to the horse."

"How much?"

"A hundred."

She stuck a hand in her pocket and pulled out five crumpled twenties.

"Much obliged. What did you say your name was?"

"Shaun."

Johnny nodded. "Right. Well, drive me there?"

They got into the truck. "It's a Shetland pony?"

"Yes."

"You plan on using it for rides?"

"Yes."

"You have to make sure it's broken or some toddler will get bucked right off. Boy or a girl?"

"Boy, but he's neutered."

Johnny laughed. "He is, is he?"

Seagn bristled. "I'm a veterinarian. I know what it looks like."

"Sorry, I'm sorry." He turned to her. "What's a vet doing with a petting zoo? I thought you'd be with the SPCA."

"I'm trying to make them healthy and to display these animals to people who never saw them."

"For free?"

"It's a dollar if they want to feed them. But, yeah, nothing to pet them."

"That's a good deal."

"I hope so. But people, you know, they always want something more."

"Heh. I know how that goes."

They pulled off Route 1 and onto the road for The Ranch. "You're out in the sticks here."

She shrugged. "Don't blame me, blame the carnival owner."

"You're a petting zoo for a carnival?"

"That's right. A traveling petting zoo."

"What kind of animals you got?"

"One horse —" As she spoke, she turned into the meadow. The carnival rides were all set up, and a black Escalade was parked among the rides. "I wonder who that is."

"Looks like the government." He pointed at the vehicle. Seagn saw US Government plates on it.

"Uh oh. Taxes," Seagn said.

"You think?"

"Who else?"

Johnny shrugged. "They here for you?"

"I hope not."

She took the left and pointed the truck away from the rides to her petting zoo. She parked the truck in front of the pen where the animals gathered.

Seagn got out of the truck. "Shet! C'mere Shet!"

The animal didn't know his name, so she had to go and fetch him from the field. Johnny stayed with the goats by the time she came back.

"You have some active goats," he said. "Mind if we do it in your trailer? I need a clean surface for him to stand on."

"Sure." She set up the ramp and led him up it. Immediately, he went to his allotted pen.

"Well trained, too," Johnny said. "Tie him up there."

"Does shoeing hurt?"

"It's like putting a pin through the tip of your fingernail. Doesn't hurt at all." He bent down and lifted each one of the hooves, studying them to see what the damage was and what he needed to do. She watched, fascinated, as he used pliers to pull the broken shoes off from the front hooves, and the solid ones from the rear hooves. Then he filed down all four of them, to Shet's irritation.

He handed the shoes to Seagn. "There you go, good as new. I'll come file 'em down every two and a half-three months, now that I know where you are."

"How much for that?"

"Fifty bucks. That's easy stuff."

She smiled at him. "Thanks for doing this for me."

"Maybe I can call you sometime if we need a quick vet checkup."

"I don't have all the tools at my disposal," she said. "I'm used to having a clinic with technology. I'm not really a country doctor."

"Maybe you have to read *All Creatures Great and Small*."
She laughed.

After dropping Johhny back off at the farm, her phone rang.

It was Liam. She put it through the truck's speakers. "Hey, kiddo."

"Hey! A traveling circus?"

"Carnival. Local carnival."

"Not local if you're traveling all over the place. Where are you going to be next?"

"I'm not sure. I have to check the schedule when I get back."

"Shaun, I have a bit of a problem."

"What's that?"

"I have to get out of the dorm in a month. That's why I was going back to Salem. I need a place to stay in the summer."

"You're not taking summer classes?"

"It's too late to register for them now. I thought I'd spend the summer with you."

She frowned. "You can stay in my place while I'm gone."

"Is that okay?"

"Sure. I'm paying for the space. I'll call my landlord and have her give you a key."

"Sweet! Thanks a bunch, Shaun."

"So pass all your classes. And do something during the summer, like get a job."

"Yeah, yeah. I knew I could depend on you. Talk to you later!"

As he hung up, she shook her head. Why didn't he tell her before? She wouldn't have pulled this stunt if she knew. But then, she wouldn't have left the practice, either.

•   •   •

Seagn pulled back into The Ranch to see the Escalade still there. This time, though, there were some rather official-looking men gathered at the RV's table. One was seated, looking through books. Two others flanked him, and Webby looked like he tried to avoid chewing his own nails. Steph showed something to the man sitting down, talking all the while.

Seagn pulled into her spot near the trailer. Now did not seem like a good time to approach Webby about where they were going this weekend. The schedule she got from Steph didn't say anything.

Seagn ended up going to Moose's truck to knock on the door. There was no answer. She walked around the truck to see everyone gathered on the opposite side of the rides, along the ridge line of trees. There were two cliques: Fatsy, Ruby, Mark, Hugo on one end; three other African men she didn't know in the middle along with Carlos and Shayna; and Joe, Maggie, and Moose on the other end, furthest away from the rides.

She walked the gauntlet of two groups to get to Moose. No one said anything to her at all. Beyond the three groups, in the woods, she could see the blue tarp of a tent.

"What's going on?" she asked.

"Inspection," said Moose.

"Who?"

"The government." Moose stood, exhaling smoke. "Since about three years ago, when the Ferris wheel on one of the local carnivals in Georgia snapped off."

"Eight people died," said Joe. "Tons of injuries."

Moose continued, "They have government inspection, state inspection, and insurance inspections."

"What about me? Don't I get inspected?"

"It's only for the rides."

"Anything a person rides on or is strapped into," Joe added.

"So, what do we do now?"

"We wait," said Moose.

"If he passes, we still have jobs. If he fails, well … you're the carnival, Shaun."

Moose grinned. "You can ask for top dollar, then."

"Can I work for you?" asked Joe, and everyone laughed.

"I'm sure he'll pass," Seagn said. Something told her that he would make sure he passes, even if bribery would be involved.

After two of Moose's chain-smoking cigarettes, they heard a car leave. Ruby and Fatsy were the first to get up, almost running to Webby's RV.

They heard the Christmas bells, and everyone got up from their chairs or the ground. "Let's see if we lost money today," said Joe.

One by one, they came out from behind the trucks and rides to approach the RV. Webby stood at the front of the RV and merely said, "We passed. You're off for the weekend." Then Webby went into the RV.

Everyone muttered. No work meant no pay. Seagn calculated the feed and the amount she would have to get to satisfy the animals. Maybe they could live on grass and water? Trimming the horse's hooves was a sudden expense. She didn't have enough food for herself now, either. And she sure as hell wasn't going to ask Ruby for anything.

She trudged back to her trailer, her mind whirling with what she'd have to pick up.

"Hey, Shaun," Moose called.

Seagn turned around.

"We were thinking of getting a motel room," he said. "There's a flea-bitten one down the road. It's not much, but it's a comfortable bed and a shower."

"Who?"

"It would be me and you, and Joe and Maggie."

"All in one room?"

He raised his hands. "I promise no hanky panky. If you want, I'll sleep on the chair and the footrest. It's a lot more comfortable than sleeping bags."

The shower sounded heavenly. "How much?"

"Twenty-five dollars. Just one night."

A hot shower for twenty-five dollars. And a real bed. The small things were so satisfying.

"You can sleep with me in the bed," said Seagn, giving him a stern look. "But I'm not having sex."

"I didn't ask that. In front of Joe and Maggie?" She thought he shuddered. "That's rude and gross."

•　　　•　　　•

The Motel 6 was a testament to its brand: just a step above flea-bitten, but way below the Hiltons of the world. Located near the Outlets in Kittery, it catered to the touristy crowd, or people who were too inebriated to get out of the Outlet restaurant territory and go home.

They played Rock-Paper-Scissors to find out who was going to get the shower first. Maggie won, so she went into the bathroom and stayed there for a good long time. Seagn watched a baseball game with the guys, mostly looking at her phone and the Internet, avoiding the hotel's free wi-fi while she looked up her banking information.

Moose was next and came out after a much shorter time.

"You used all the hot water," he complained. He didn't have a shirt, and Seagn tried not to stare at his chest. Not quite six-pack abs, but he did have broad pecs and strong arms. With his hair wet and no longer greasy, he looked less like a hippie and more like a human.

Seagn and Joe waited a few hours before taking their own showers. In the meantime, they ordered pizza and watched TV. Seagn played Solitaire on her phone.

Seagn went in the shower and luxuriated in the hot water and steamy soak. She washed her hair with the soap as there was no more shampoo left. The towels were still damp, but she dried off the best she could before changing into new clothes.

She came out saying, "We need new towels."

"I'll go get them," said Moose and left the room.

"Did you leave me hot water?" asked Joe.

"I tried."

It was late before they finally settled down for bed. "I'll sleep on the chair," said Moose.

"No, I meant what I said," Seagn protested, even while she felt her face burn hot.

Moose smiled. "Really. I insist."

Joe butted in, "He doesn't want his woody waking you up."

Now it was Moose's turn to blush while laughing. "Just give me a blanket."

Seagn gave him the blanket, while she kept the sheet and coverlet. Joe shut the light off and Seagn settled in. She didn't fall asleep right away. She heard the sleeping sounds of the other three and turned to stare at the ceiling.

What the hell am I doing? The bed was too big, and to have Moose next to her would be a comforting thing. She sat up and looked over in the dim light to see Moose, sleeping soundly.

She shrugged, turned over. *Well, you blew that opportunity.*

10

"OH GOOD. GRASS."

Seagn smiled when she saw the large field they would set up in. The day dawned nice, and the weekend here was going to be beautiful — sunny, in the high sixties. At this local festival, food vendors with portable grills had already set up in a section off to the side. The animals were going to be on the farthest end of the exhibits, across from "Authors' Row" — a series of tables with books and their authors.

"Hopefully not Japanese grass," said Moose as he pulled into the spot the handlers directed him into.

Seagn chuckled at that.

One of the handlers came up to the truck. "After you unload, you have to park the trailer down the road."

"How far down the road?"

"A mile or so in the Wal-Mart parking lot."

They weren't quite in the middle of the sticks. The field was off a busy two-lane road, with many box-stores surrounding it.

The RV had to park at Wal-Mart as well. Webby expressed his annoyance at that once they shut off the trucks.

Seagn got out of the truck to examine the terrain. There were large stones under the crabby grass, like this had been a ruin of a large store that had given up to the elements. It was uneven and rocky, but she knew the animals would get used to it.

However, her trailer was a mile away. There was no way she could herd the goats down a busy street back to the trailer. She would have to stay with the animals under the tent overnight.

Luckily, she had purchased a nylon folding chair with an optional footrest. She could sleep in one of the pens, probably with Bella, as she was not usually excitable when Seagn went into her pen.

First the tent, then the fencing, then the lighting. Moose manhandled the generator out of the truck — she didn't even know it could come out — and set it up out of the way. It would make noise, but then, all of the rides needed generators, so there would be a constant humming and thrumming of noise at night.

Last, the animals. Herded quietly into their pens, they settled down to taste the grass.

Seagn looked over the pens and smiled. This was going to be a nice set-up. Not crowded at all. She unloaded bags of food and jugs of water for the weekend and set up a disposing station with a trash bag. She also set up her folding chair.

An official with a lanyard came by as she used her dolly to bring out the feed. "Excuse me," he called.

"Yes?" She stopped, brushing her hands on her jeans.

"I'm from the Rhode Island Tax Office. Are you selling anything?"

"Why?"

"Because it's taxable."

That meant she couldn't sell feed. "No," she said. "You can pet the animals. It's free."

"They got their rabies shots?"

The color drained from Seagn's face. Though Fatsy said he did, could she really trust him?

The tax official said, his hands up, "Just asking. That's not my job."

"They don't bite." At least recently they hadn't. The goats were a little pushy, but none of them had bitten anyone. Yet.

She assumed they didn't get *any* shots: rabies, HIV, flu, not to mention species-specific shots that she'd have to look into. *Where am I going to get the medicine?*

Seagn tried not to panic. The idea of an inspection got her nervous. She believed someone somewhere was going to report her for cruelty because of the present state of the animals. Although healthier than they were when she first bought them, they were still somewhat in wretched condition.

She looked over the rambunctious goats. *I'm helping them. Wouldn't they be better on a farm?*

"Don't start," she said to herself, as she plugged the lights into the generator. Sundown would be here soon, and the carnival would be lit up, ready for business.

Seagn watched attentively as people pet the animals, laughing and giggling at their antics, having a good time. Seagn still had a bad feeling about all this. *Who would report me?*

That night, she set up her chair in the pen with Bella, who lay down to sleep without any fuss.

Moose came over to the pen. "Hey, I'm going back to the trucks. Do you need anything for tomorrow?"

"More water. Use the dolly." She handed him the key to the lock.

"You know, you probably don't have to sleep here."

"I don't feel comfortable leaving them out like this."

"Fatsy did it all the time."

"I'm not Fatsy."

Moose inclined his head and gave her a genuine smile. "True, that. Well, I'll see you tomorrow."

•   •   •

Her bad feeling didn't go away the next day when the festival was in full swing. Were the animals angry? Would they bite anyone? Would some toddler grab a goat's beard and tug, pissing off the goat and making it attack? Would someone kick the pigs?

By sundown, she was so wound up that she was tempted to close the pens off from people and their kids. She hadn't eaten, hadn't left except for quick bathroom breaks. She constantly watched the animals and the people around them. She had cleaned up after them, made sure their troughs were full of water, and took her time feeding them, making it obvious to anyone who watched that she was giving them the right food.

"Excuse me," someone called while she filled an area with hay for the sheep. "Are these your animals?"

She turned to see a young woman in an off-the-shoulder shirt and shorts, even though it was still too cool for shorts.

"Yes," Seagn said.

"I'm Tina from the RISPCA."

Seagn let out the breath she'd been holding all day. "Is there anything wrong?"

"No." The woman smiled. "In fact, this is a really nice set-up. Better than the one I saw last year."

She knew that part was true. "I'm the new owner. A much better owner. A veterinarian." She held out her hand. "Shaun Conway."

Tina shook Seagn's hand. "They have plenty of room and seem contented. The goats are cute."

"Want to play with them?"

"It looks like they just ate."

"That never stopped them before. Come on in."

Seagn opened the gate and let Tina into the pen. At seeing another person, they immediately gathered around her. Tina laughed and rubbed the rough hair on their foreheads. When they realized this person wasn't giving them food, three out of the five went back to the feeding area, while the other two who were a little more dense stayed with Tina.

"Everything's all right?" Seagn asked.

"I've seen some farms in worse condition. You're providing a service, right? To bring the farm to the city."

Seagn's heart swelled. Someone who understood! "Yes. Exactly that."

Tina stepped away from the goats, who insisted on following her to the gate. "They're so cute."

"Thank you," Seagn said.

She examined Tina a little more closely. She looked to be in her twenties, around Seagn's age. She stood about Seagn's height, with deep blue eyes, and a long auburn hair tied back in a functional ponytail. Her skin was tanned already this early in the season.

"Well, I'd better go. You probably still have to feed them, right?"

"Just Bella."

"Oh! They all have names?"

"Of course they do."

Seagn pointed them out and told her their names. Tina laughed at the Golden Girls reference for the sheep.

"They look well-cared for," said Tina. "Can I get you anything from the food court?"

Seagn tucked her hand in her jeans pocket, fishing for money. "I'd like —"

"No. My treat."

"You sure?"

"Sure, I'm sure. It's the least I could do with what you're doing with the animals."

"Okay, then … can you get me a sausage and pepper sandwich from the blue vendor truck. Only from him. I don't know what he does, but his sandwiches are the best."

"I'll get one too. Anything to drink?"

"Lemonade if you can find it. Oh, and a funnel cake."

"Sausage and pepper sandwich, funnel cake, and lemonade. Got it."

"It's going to cost you a lot."

Tina waved her hand as she walked away. "It's worth it."

Seagn smiled as Tina left. All of her worries about the inspection of the animals melted away. If the SPCA approved, then she was all set.

At around eight, Moose came over. Tina hadn't returned. Seagn's stomach rumbled mightily.

"A little hungry, are we?" Moose said.

"My errand girl hasn't come back yet."

"Did you pay her already?"

"No."

"I was going to say, never pay the errand boy beforehand. They always steal your money."

Seagn frowned. "It's been more than an hour."

"Want me to get you something?"

She looked toward the midway and thought she saw Tina. It wasn't, because the woman wasn't carrying anything.

"No, I'll be all right."

"You'll have a sugar drop if you don't eat anything."

Seagn pulled out a five. "Get me a doughboy. Please."

Moose took it and went off on his quest. Then, about ten minutes later, Tina returned.

"I'm so sorry! I couldn't carry everything, so I ate my sandwich, then I saw some girls from high school and we got to talking …"

Seagn took the cold sandwich, the wilted funnel cake, and the watered-down lemonade. "It's fine."

"I have to go because the girls are going to go on The Spinner."

"It's okay. Thanks." She tried not to sound snippy or angry, but it might have come across in her body language, because Tina looked down and whirled around.

She bumped right into Moose.

"Oh! Excuse me."

Moose only gave her a grunt, as he usually did with people who irritated him. He had two doughboys in his hand.

"Sorry," Tina said, and took off.

Seagn sighed.

"Better than nothing," Moose said.

She sipped the lemonade. Definitely watered-down.

Moose sat on the hay bale that Seagn was using for feed. "So how has it been going?"

"Pretty busy. That girl was in the SPCA. She approved the set-up."

"That girl?"

"Yeah." Seagn bit into the sausage and pepper sandwich and almost moaned at how good it was, even cold.

"That wasn't the SPCA. They come in suits."

She paused in her chewing, swallowed. "Then who …?"

Moose brushed sugar from his mustache as he said, "Dunno. But you gonna stop worrying now?"

"Was it obvious?"

"When I mentioned inspection, you got white as a ghost. Don't worry, it's just a yearly thing."

"I'm still going to have to give them shots. Just to be safe." She bit into the sandwich. Not quite cold and greasy, but not exactly fresh, either. "How am I going to get them?"

"Order them to your house?"

"That's not how it works. It has to be ordered by a clinic."

"What about your old clinic?"

"I didn't exactly leave on the best of terms. They probably removed me from the staff within minutes of my walking out."

He drank his soda. "Better to beg forgiveness than ask permission."

She turned to him. "What was that?"

"Order the stuff, and then go down and pick it up. Apologize that you did it, but it was for the sake of the animals. Pay for it ahead of time so they don't freak out that you're using company funds."

"Moose, you're brilliant."

He laughed. "Ain't ever heard that before."

She pulled out her phone. "I can order everything online and deliver it to the clinic and pick it up next week. You are absolutely brilliant."

He brushed away the powdered sugar that had fallen on his pants from the doughboy. "Glad I could help."

Seagn didn't notice when Moose got up and left, so concentrated she was on her phone. After several minutes of searching, the Internet told her what shots to get for each species, and she ordered them all, using her phone wallet to pay for it. By the time she looked up from her phone, the zoo was full of people, and she hadn't cleaned.

But the people didn't care, it seemed, petting the animals and marveling at the miniature size of Shet and Bob's broken horn. She smiled. Everything was going to be okay.

•   •   •

Seagn hummed a jaunty tune while she fed the animals on Sunday morning before opening. She had slept better than the night before, even when she was covered in dew after she woke up. She planned on sleeping the day away on Monday to catch up for her fitful sleep over the past few days.

The carnival opened without a hitch. It was overcast and a little chilly for the middle of May.

She left the animals to go to the bathroom and, when she returned, three people in fancy Sunday clothes stood near her chair. "Hello?" she asked.

"Are you in charge here?" one of the dark-skinned men said to her.

"Yes," she said.

The man took out lanyard from his pocket. "SPCA. We have a report that your animals are in sub-standard conditions."

"What? Someone came by yesterday and said they were fine."

The two men and woman looked at each other. To Seagn, they looked like Puritans, with their dark clothes and formal demeanor. "No one from our office came here yesterday."

"Sure, she did. Tina."

The woman shook her head. "No one is in our office by that name."

Moose was right. "Someone came by yesterday and said —"

"Did they show you ID?"

She thought back. "Um, no ..."

The man who hadn't spoken yet said, "We can see that these animals are not given the freedom to roam together."

"It's easier for people to have them separate. The goats, they get rambunctious, and the sheep are nervous —"

"We heard that you didn't give them enough room to lie down," said the dark-skinned man. "We see that's been rectified."

"That was last year. The guy who owned them didn't take care of them."

"Are they being fed?"

"Twice a day. Appropriate feed for their species."

"Do you have any paperwork on these animals?"

Said the woman, "Such as vaccinations, where you got them, how much you paid for them."

Seagn stammered to explain. "I don't know, but I just ordered their vaccinations and planned on picking them up this week." *Fatsy, I hate you.*

"Where?"

"Salem. Central Avenue Veterinary Clinic. I worked there until about two months ago."

"Do you have their number?"

At the same time, the other man asked, "What did you do there?"

She turned to the woman and rattled off the number. Then she said, "I was one of the vets there." Seagn glanced at the animals obliviously eating from the troughs in their pens. *What a stupid idea to buy this ... what was I thinking — saving a few goats and sheep?*

"Do you still have your license to practice?"

"It's in the truck, a mile away down the street."

"We'll take you to go get it."

The dark-skinned man said, "Do you carry drugs for these animals in case of emergency?"

"Yes," Seagn replied. "And I have the permits."

"For Massachusetts. Do you have them for Rhode Island?"

"I need a permit to have the drugs in Rhode Island?"

"Yes, because some are fit for human consumption."

"You mean the Mass one doesn't cover it?"

"Not in Rhode Island."

"We have some different drugs on the list," said the woman.

"Will you be in Rhode Island again?" asked the man.

"I'll have to check."

"We'll check on your permits when we see you next."

The dark-skinned man looked back at the animals. "In the meantime, you can display them, but not let people touch them. They haven't been vaccinated."

"They're not safe," said the woman.

Seagn watched as the three of them glanced into the pens before leaving. Seagn knew she couldn't stop everyone from petting the animals, especially kids sticking their hands in the cages as they usually did.

"Sorry, guys," she said over and over to people who reached in to try and pet the animals. "You can't touch."

Around the middle of the day, Webby waddled himself down to her area.

"What's going on?" he demanded.

"SPCA came over and told me I can't let people pet the animals until they get their shots."

"You're a vet. Give 'em to them."

"I have to order them." She held up her phone. "I have to deliver them to Salem and pick them up next week."

"Why Salem?"

"They're drugs. Some are fit for human consumption. Someone has to sign for them."

"I thought you said they couldn't be used by people?"

Seagn paused in her answer. Ruby must've told Fatsy, who told Webby what she had said a few days ago. "Not if you give a person what an animal normally takes. Horses are bigger than people, and cats are smaller than people. You could mess up and overdose or underdose."

Webby frowned. At least he didn't yell at her. "They'll be ready for next week?"

"Certainly. I ordered it express."

"As long as they can pet 'em, that'll be fine. It's a petting zoo, not a farm display." He glared at the animals, as if it was their fault. Then he left.

Seagn sighed. She couldn't wait until it was time for them to close.

11

ON TUESDAY AFTERNOON, Seagn got a call from the clinic. She took a breath and sat down in her folding chair. She kept an eye on the animals, who were all lazing about in the spring air.

"Hello?" Seagn hoped that it was someone on staff. She had a good relationship with the staff at the clinic.

"Shaun," said Hailey. "What's going on?"

"Hi, Hailey!" She forced herself to smile, hoping that would carry over the phone. "I guess you got my packages?"

"What are you doing?"

"I'm vaccinating these animals. I put it on my card."

"Can't you deliver it to where you are now?"

"I'm not at a clinic."

Hailey exhaled. "This is the first and last time you're going to do this. We're not your PO box."

"I'll be there first thing tomorrow morning to pick it all up."

"They're taking up room in the fridge. You better be here by this time tomorrow or I'm tossing it all out."

"I'll be there. I appreciate it. Thanks so much."

"Hmpf." She hung up.

Seagn turned to Bella, who had come up to her at the fence. "Well, that wasn't too bad." She scratched Bella's forehead. "I think I'm getting used to people screaming at me."

Shayna suddenly came over from where everyone else had been camped. Seagn waved to her. She paused, looked at Seagn, then the animals. She said something in Spanish and smiled.

"I don't speak Spanish," she said.

Shayna pointed to herself, then the animals. She made a petting motion with her hand.

"Oh, sure, you can pet them." Seagn got up and opened the gate, waving her inside.

Shayna walked over to the sheep that lay in the sun. Rose *baaed* at her while Dorothy stretched out on the grass. Shayna giggled.

Seagn felt the same warm happiness that she did when she saw kids with the animals. Shayna ran her hands through Dorothy's fleece, saying something to Seagn. Seagn shrugged.

She heard Carlos call from the firepit. "Shayna!" He turned in her direction. He inclined his head and came over to the trailer.

Shayna said something in Spanish to him. Carlos said, "She's been wanting to touch your sheep since you are here. They remind her of home."

"I'm glad."

"*Bueno.* It's good."

Shayna lay her head on the sheep's stomach. Dorothy didn't move. Rose didn't like it, so butted her head into Shayna's side. This got the goats moving, and they bounced over to Shayna, jumping on her. Carlos laughed at them, at Shayna trying to get up and shoo them away. She let out a string of Spanish, which made Carlos laugh harder. That caused Seagn to laugh. Carlos doubled over laughing, the animals got more active with the pigs coming into the picture.

When Seagn could catch her breath, she saw Moose heading across the meadow, a look of confusion on his face. Carlos straightened, tears in his eyes from laughing so hard. Shayna had gotten herself disengaged from the sheep, goats, pigs — and soon-to-be horse. She dashed to the gate, the animals chasing her.

Seagn helped open the gate and Shayna ran out. She playfully hit Carlos, who still laughed at her. They said some things to each other in Spanish, and Carlos led Shayna away.

Moose approached Seagn. "What was all that?"

Seagn leaned on her knees, breathing heavily, and smiling. "America's Funniest Home Videos."

•　　•　　•

Boston traffic was horrible, as usual. She had to take I-95 south to Salem, which was north of the city, but it had already started backing up in Danvers. Luckily, she had filled the little truck's tank and found a good rock station on the radio.

She got to the clinic a half hour after it opened: 9:30 in the morning. The waiting room was empty, but she could hear barking in the recesses of the exam rooms in the back.

"Shaun!" Elizabeth, a heavyset older woman who had been there almost as long as Seagn, waved from the area blocked off for the doctors' desks. She walked over, pulling the two-way half-door that separated the counter from the waiting room, and gave Seagn a hug.

"We've missed you."

"I've missed you, too. Is Hailey around?"

"She's with a patient."

"I'd like to try and avoid her, if possible."

"Then you'd better hurry up. Are you working somewhere else?"

"Kind of. I own a carnival side show now. Petting zoo."

"A what, now?"

"Horses and goats and sheep, oh my."

"That's why I never heard of some of those medicines."

"Let's go get them and I'll get out before Hailey's done."

Elizabeth led the way to the fridge. "They're all on the door."

Seagn opened the door to see it chock full of vials and boxes which contained vials. Elizabeth took down the box of needles Seagn had ordered while she packed the vials into another box. She would have to dispose of the needles at a pharmacy. Once out of the fridge, she had 30 days to use the vaccines. Most were for Shet and Bella.

Elizabeth put the packing slip with the vaccines. "There you —"

A door opened, and Seagn heard the scratching of a dog on the tiles as it tried to get away from a leash. "Just check out at the desk," called Hailey. "Give me a minute to update the records."

"Thanks, Doctor," said a man, who came around the corner with a bulldog dragging him to the front desk. He waved at Seagn. "Hey, Doc! Haven't seen you around."

"Oh, I left the practice," Seagn said.

Hailey peered around the corner of the exam room. "Shaun? If you'd wait a minute."

Seagn's stomach dropped to her shoes. She looked to Elizabeth, who bowed her head and went to the front desk. Seagn prepared herself for a confrontation.

Hailey came out of the exam room, wiping her hands together, obviously having used the hand sanitizer found in every room. She frowned, her face crumpled up in suppressed fury. That face meant a yelling match, Seagn knew from experience.

"You've got some nerve," Hailey said, as Seagn looked out at the front desk, Elizabeth and the man concentrating entirely on each other to ignore what was going to happen.

"I know, I should have called you—"

"Where did you go? What practice that doesn't have you on their payroll, huh?"

"I joined a carnival."

"What? Why?"

"They had a petting zoo. The animals were in rough shape. I wanted to take care of them."

"What animals? Big cats?"

"No, farm animals. A Shetland pony and a small cow, some sheep —"

"You don't know anything about farm animals!"

"How do you know? All you do here is cats and dogs, and the occasional lizard and rabbit."

The front door opened and shut, as the man got out before things got even more heated.

"You never did farm animals."

"That doesn't mean I don't know them."

Hailey threw her hands up in the air. "I can't believe you gave up a lucrative practice to be a carnival barker."

"I wanted to help the animals. Isn't that what we do?"

Hailey tugged her ponytail. Seagn waited. Hailey paused.

"Well?"

"Not at my expense," Hailey stated.

"I put that all on my phone. You're not responsible for any of it."

"I'm responsible for it once it comes into my door. You had no right to do that."

"You know I can't send it to anything but a vet's."

"Find a vet with the carnival. Or something else. Don't use here."

"I won't. Not anymore."

Hailey snorted, like she did when she was frustrated. "Take your stuff and get out. Don't come back."

Elizabeth bowed her head as Seagn picked up the boxes and showed herself the door.

•   •   •

Seagn had just crossed the border into New Hampshire when she saw a biker gang gathered on the side of the road.

It wasn't just any gang. It was a group of women gathered around a motorcycle.

She pulled over, then backed up to them. She got out of the truck and started to approach.

They all wore black leather jackets, jeans, and t-shirts. The back of the leather jacket had a "Don't Tread On Me" snake symbol on it. Above it was the word "Sidewinders", and below it, "Arizona". A gray-haired woman with spiky short hair walked out of the pack of women to greet Seagn. "You from Laconia?"

"No," Seagn said. "Kittery. What's wrong?"

"One of our bikes died."

She looked at the bikes. They were mostly big and bulky Harleys. "Need a phone to call Triple-A?"

The gray-haired woman laughed. "They don't tow bikes."

"Can you fit it on my truck?"

The woman looked around Seagn to where the truck was parked. "I think so. Can your truck handle it?"

"We'll find out, right?"

The woman turned around and yelled at the group, "Taurus! Blinky! C'mon, we got a ride."

The two women who approached Seagn looked like weightlifters. Another woman pushed a bike out of the pack and negotiated it around the other parked bikes. It was smaller than the rest and looked like it could fit. But how were they going to get it on the truck without a ramp?

Blinky seemed to be named that because she kept blinking her eyes as she talked. "We got it," she said.

Taurus, the other weightlifter, stood on the truck's bed. Blinky lifted the bike by the front wheel and then lifted its back wheel, while Taurus guided the bike into the middle of the bed. The truck sank a little.

"Got any — no, I see some," said Taurus, gathering rope from the back of the truck. There were also some bungee cords that she also used to secure the bike in place. Taurus jumped down and nodded to Seagn.

"I'm Gray," said the woman, holding her hand out to Seagn.

"Shaun."

"Can you give us a ride to Laconia?"

"Sure."

"Go ahead, Sheila. Ride with Shaun here. Follow us."

"We have to get on 93," said Sheila as she got into the cab of the truck. Sheila was of average height and build, easily her brother's age. The bikes all roared to life and pulled out as a group onto the highway. Seagn followed at the tail end of them.

Seagn turned to Sheila. "You guys are from Arizona?"

"Yeah. We thought we'd come up for Memorial Day weekend."

Seagn turned down the radio so they could talk. "I never saw a group of female motorcyclists before."

Sheila huffed. "Totally not surprising."

From Interstate 95, they took Route 101 to get to Interstate 93.

Seagn asked, "You come up this way every year?"

"Yeah." Sheila leaned back in the seat. "So what do you do?"

"I'm a veterinarian in charge of a mobile petting zoo."

"That's way cool! Like freakshow full of animals and stuff?"

Seagn chuckled. "They're farm animals. Goats, sheep, a cow."

Her text chime went off and the truck read it to her. "Hey sis I need to come to Salem by May 18 can I come."

Sheila looked to Seagn. "You gonna answer that?"

"I don't know if the truck can reply. This is a Tacoma."

"It's Japanese. They were smart."

Seagn pressed the button on the steering wheel to activate the voice-command system. "Reply to text."

Pause.

"Please say one of the following: Reply to recent text. Call back nay—"

Oh, for heaven's … "Reply to recent text."

"Replying to recent text. Begin." A beep chimed.

"I'm driving. Will text when I'm done."

The truck beeped again, probably at the word "done". "Text sent."

Sheila chuckled. "Isn't technology amazing?"

"When it works."

Sheila laughed. "How many farm animals do you have?"

Seagn counted in her head. "Eleven."

She went into detail, naming each animal as Sheila counted on her fingers. She didn't mention Tommy, though it hurt her a little not to. She explained, again, why she bought the animals.

"You got one of those Hypocratic Oaths?"

"Hippocratic Oath. Yes, we take a Veterinary Oath. We protect animals and alleviate their suffering."

"Are they suffering in a petting zoo?"

"They were. That's why I bought them. The guy taking care of them didn't care."

A car tried to pass on the right, to get in front of the truck, and squeeze into the lane. Seagn closed up the gap. The car beeped long and loud.

"Asshole," Seagn muttered.

"Not surprising," said Sheila. "They do this stuff to us all the time."

The car dropped back behind Seagn and beeped again to show the driver's irritation.

"Too bad for them," Seagn said. "They can pass the group if they think we're slow. And we're not. We're going just about the speed limit."

"So fuck 'em."

Seagn chuckled. "My thoughts exactly."

The car came up on the right again, passing Seagn and heading into the pack.

"Shit, look at that!" Sheila sat up straight in her chair.

The women split, and enveloped the car, with two bikes on the side of it. Then they all went slower. The car kept hitting the horn and its brakes. The bikes all put their hazards on, so Seagn put hers on as well. Finally, one of the women gave the car room to dart out and take off down the highway. Sheila laughed.

"It's too bad you're used to it."

"It's worse if it's a bunch of guys. They like to try and slip between us and run us off the road."

"You're all women?"

"Yes."

"How come?"

Sheila gave her a sly glance. "We like women."

"Ohhhh."

"What do you think of us now that we're dykes?"

"I don't have a problem with it. But my last relationship was with a younger girl. I don't want to go down that path again."

Sheila waved a hand in dismissal. "I wouldn't ask you. I already have a girl. She's fourth from the back."

"You're not riding with her?"

"What? I have my own bike."

"I thought that girlfriends rode —"

"You've been watching way too many biker movies. We believe in independence. You bring your own bike."

They passed a few strip malls, then the area around them became more residential. Seagn asked, "So your leader is this Gray person?"

"I guess you could say 'leader'. But we don't ask her permission for everything. She's more of a guide. Does your radio work?"

"Yeah, just AM/FM. You wouldn't want to listen to my playlist on the phone."

"Is it classical music?"

Seagn laughed. "Classic rock."

"Let me see your phone, I'll get it started."

Sheila connected the phone to the Bluetooth and soon "Bad Company" blared from the speakers.

•   •   •

Like Salem was a mecca for witches, Laconia was the same for bikers. Seagn could tell as they pulled into the city limits. Motorcycle shops, repair shops, and gift stores were everywhere.

"A themed tourist trap, like Salem," said Seagn, as she followed the line of bikers slowly down the street.

Gray broke from the pack and waited for Seagn to catch up. In the middle of the street, she called to her, "Follow me!"

Seagn followed Gray down the street a couple of blocks from where the women had parked their bikes. She found herself pulling up in front of a garage door.

Gray parked her bike just outside the main entrance. She went inside.

"We always come here," said Sheila. "The only woman-owned repair shop in town." She bopped her head to "My Sharona" playing in the truck.

The garage door in front of her opened, and a man came out carrying a ramp. Seagn shut off the truck and got out.

"Afternoon," said the man with a nod.

Seagn took down the tailgate and the man set up the ramp. He undid the knots on the ropes, then guided the bike down the ramp.

Gray stepped out with a woman wearing a Bike Week t-shirt from three years ago. "I'll get working on her right away," she said. "Put it on your tab?"

"If you could," said Gray, watching the man roll the bike into the shop. "Thanks a lot."

"Anytime, Gray. Staying for the weekend?"

"Yeah." She turned to Seagn. "Want to give Sheila a ride back to the hotel?"

"Sure thing."

The few blocks didn't take long and, as soon as she turned the truck off, Sheila was out of the cab. "Thanks for the ride!"

"Yep!" Seagn waved her away.

Gray came up to Seagn's driver's side. "Is there anything I can do to repay you?"

"This might sound crazy, but can I take a shower?"

Gray smirked. "Alone, or with someone?"

"Alone, please."

"I don't see why not. I'll let you use mine."

The bed and breakfast seemed to be taken up by everyone in the group. Gray had the entire top floor, with slanted ceilings and her own bathroom.

"This is the Mistress Suite. Or Master Suite during Bike Week."

The decorations were Victorian — daguerreotypes of mysterious men and women dressed up in fancy gilded frames. An ancient wardrobe stood in the only section where the ceiling was high enough to fit it. The bed was at the end of the room, set off with Chinese room dividers. The bathroom had a full-sized frosted window looking out toward the expansive lawn at the back of the house.

"Take your time. I'll be downstairs."

Seagn did take her time. She was happy her clothes were clean from this morning. She could wear them for a couple of days before she felt uncomfortable. Some of the carnies wore their clothes for an entire week, sleeping in them as well. She tried not to go that far.

She walked downstairs, her hair still wet. She felt refreshed and clean. The group of women were smoking or just sitting around the lobby. The TV was on, but too low for her to hear. Sheila stood up and started to applaud.

The rest of the group applauded, and Seagn felt her face get hot. She bowed her head. "Thank you."

"Want to stick around?" asked Gray. "We're going to dinner."

"I'd love to, but I have to get back to my animals."

"Yeah, Sheila said something about a carnival. Where are you going to be this weekend?"

"Narragansett. It's in Rhode Island."

"That's a long ways away. Maybe we'll catch up with you sometime."

"I don't have the schedule with me —"

"Want to exchange digits?" Gray pulled out her phone.

Seagn pulled out hers, and tapped the two together, like toasting someone. A pleasant little chirp notified them they had transferred their phone numbers to each other.

Gray looked at her phone. "That's a weird spelling of your name."

"It's supposed to be Gaelic." Seagn looked at hers. *Gray Miller, Company: Sidewinders, AZ.*

"Call and let us know where you'll be. We'll be in the area for a couple of months."

"Laconia?"

She laughed. "New England. Compared to Arizona, it's a county."

"My schedule is ever-changing. I usually don't know where I'll be until a couple of days before."

"That's okay. This is New England. Anything is an hour away."

"Heh, true. Well, thanks for the shower. I hope to see you again."

Gray kissed Seagn on the cheek. "Be careful, huh?"

Seagn stiffened. She stepped back, touched her cheek. Gray only smiled at her.

"I will," Seagn said while her face got hot. "Thanks."

12

I T WAS DARK WHEN SEAGN FINALLY GOT TO MAINE, so she had to pick her way to the road leading to The Ranch. Landmarks weren't clear by the headlights of the truck, and she found herself going down a couple of dirt tracks that ended in a house or a decrepit barn.

She finally came upon the canopy of forest that preceded The Ranch. When she saw the cooking fire in the distance, she let out a sigh of relief. The truck bounced its way out of the forest and turned left to park at the trailer.

The goats were beside themselves, running over to the fence and bleating at her to feed them.

They weren't the only ones. Moose showed up with a flashlight just as she parked the truck. "Where have you been?"

"Salem. With a side stop at Laconia."

"How'd that happen?"

She smiled. "I'll tell you later."

"Need help feeding them?"

"Could you hold the flashlight?" She didn't want to waste fuel on the generator and string up lights.

After feeding the animals, Seagn told Moose what had happened.

Moose smoked another cigarette and pondered the adventure. "Lesbian biker gang, huh?"

"Yeah, I guess you could call them that."

"Sounds like a porno flick in the making."

Seagn hit him playfully. "They were very respectful. Not what you think."

Moose rubbed his arm. "I'm just kidding. Though if it were me, I would have stayed."

"I have responsibilities. Tomorrow all the animals are all getting their shots."

"Rabies?"

"And distemper. And a few others. Shet is the most expensive." She looked around the trailer. "Have you seen Maisey?"

"Which one's that?"

"The cat."

"I haven't seen it around here."

"I haven't seen her since Warwick."

"Think she ran off?"

"God, I hope not. She's chipped, though, so whoever brings her to the vet will find out she's mine."

"That is, if someone brings her to the vet."

Seagn frowned deeply. "Yeah. There is that. I'll look for her tomorrow morning."

"After shooting up the goats?"

She chuckled. "After that."

The next morning, she lined up the vials on the trailer's edge and filled syringes with the required amount as shown on a special veterinarian's web page she had access to. She went down the line, giving each animal a shot behind its neck. No one complained.

It took her about an hour, and then she had breakfast: Pop Tarts and Sunny D. In the back of her mind was Maisey. What if she did run off in Warwick? How was she going to find her?

She started making calls, to the Rhode Island SPCA, to the Warwick Animal Shelter. Maybe someone would show up with her and give her up to the shelter. Or, God forbid, she went feral and joined a colony.

For funsies, she looked through the trailer. With the exception of animal crap, no Maisey. No traces of mice, either. She'd done her job and moved on, Seagn thought, although that didn't make her feel any better.

• • •

Although they were on a highway, it was strange to see old historic farms along the side of the road on their way to Narragansett. According to Seagn's GPS, Narragansett was on the water. When they pulled into the spot, which turned out to be a football-sized field, it was just across the street from a beach. A pair of stone towers that seemed to have no reason to be there supported a stone bridge between them over the main road.

Webby pulled out all the stops here, bringing every single ride and all the members of the crew. Everything from the carousel to the Ferris wheel was brought in. The trucks had to park down the road, so Seagn found herself loading feed for the weekend into a small section of the tent. She was also far away from the beach and the Midway, the section where the rides were showcased. She'd learned the term from Moose on their way in.

They were packed in tight, with barely enough room to move around. If the SPCA was going to inspect her this weekend, she was going to be in big trouble.

Seagn set up the animals with the maximum amount of space she could fit. She got dirty looks from the guys setting up the Swinger, because her tent barely cleared the arc of the swing. Webby let it stand because it was more threatening to the people on the swings.

After setting up, she called the shelters again. No tuxedo cat had been recently found.

"Maybe she's in the woods," Seagn said out of nowhere, as Moose strung up the lighting.

"Who?"

Seagn shook her head. "Maisey. Sorry. Still thinking about her."

"She probably took off with some handsome stray in Warwick."

"She's spayed."

"Doesn't mean she don't have needs."

Seagn rolled her eyes. "Right. I wouldn't know anything about that."

"So about that group you met up with …"

"Every man's wet dream?"

Moose didn't even blush. "Not me. Were you interested in any of them?"

"No. I'm not interested in that at all."

"The last girl must have really burned you."

Seagn sighed.

"Okay, I won't talk about it anymore."

"Please. I have to concentrate on these guys."

"What is there to concentrate on? They look fine."

"The SPCA doesn't think so."

Moose came down from the ladder. "You didn't say anything about that. Why didn't you tell Webby?"

"Because it's not his problem."

"It is if you can't set up."

"I already gave them their shots. But if they show up today, things are kinda tight."

"It's Memorial Day Weekend. They won't show up."

"That doesn't matter. They might show up *because* it's Memorial Day Weekend."

Moose put a hand on her shoulder. "Stop worrying. You've done what you can do."

Seagn hunched her shoulders. "I know. I hope I pass this time."

Night fell, and Seagn passed out bags of feed to people for free. That way she wouldn't have to feed the animals late at night. She asked for the bags back to reuse, but most of the time people left them on the grass for her to pick up.

Steph came over in a surprise visit. "You got a lot of people here."

"I guess there's no farms around."

"That's not true. There's one on the island."

Seagn didn't respond.

"So, what's this about the SPCA?"

"How did word get to you?"

"Moose might have mentioned it. I hope you don't expect us to pay for anything."

"I wasn't going to ask."

Steph shrugged. "Good, because this is all you."

She left, and Seagn glared across the Midway at the motorcycle ride that Moose usually manned.

When things started to die down, around nine o'clock, Seagn stormed across the Midway to Moose. No one was on his ride, so he was trying to sneak a cigarette.

"You blabbermouth," she yelled at him.

"What did I do now?"

"You told Steph about the SPCA?"

"Hey." He raised his hands. "I'm only trying to help."

"She came over and said it's all my responsibility. Which I already knew."

"They should at least give you something."

"Are you kidding? Look at where I am. I'm the last thing on the Midway. I'm an afterthought. They probably were planning on killing all the animals anyway, which is why Fatsy had them."

"Fatsy's the supe now," Moose said.

Someone approached for the ride.

"Excuse me," he said, and opened the gate for the woman and a little girl.

Seagn smiled at her. The little girl gave her a grin, as if she was going to do something that wasn't allowed.

If she only knew, Seagn thought with a smile, going back to her spot.

•　　•　　•

An hour later, everything closed except for the bars along the beach. Moose and Joe came over. Maggie was nowhere to be seen.

"Where's Maggie?"

"She got her period," said Joe. "She's back at The Ranch."

Seagn rolled her eyes. "It's not like having your period is a sickness."

"With her it is." Joe bristled.

Moose said, "I told you she just uses it as an excuse."

Seagn nodded. "She is."

"You don't live with her. Anyway, we're not talking about Maggie. I got a draw so we can go to the bar."

Seagn knew that a "draw" meant an advance from his paycheck. "You paying?"

"One round."

"Okay. I'll have a Coke on you. But I have to be back soon."

Joe slapped her on the back. "On me."

They walked to the nearest bar, only two blocks away. The parking lot was full and the place was crowded. When they found their way to the bar, Seagn ordered a Coke; Moose and Joe both ordered Corona without limes. They ambled to an empty table with no chairs.

"What's this about the SPCA?" asked Joe over the ambient noise.

"Did you tell everyone?" Seagn glared at Moose.

"Only the ones who cared."

"Does Fatsy know?"

"Probably now, yeah."

"Great. Like I need him to stick his nose into my business."

Moose drank half the bottle at once. "He won't say nothing to you."

Seagn frowned. "I'll believe it when I see it."

The next thing she knew, it was last call. Moose and Joe had drunk a few, so were feeling no pain.

"We're gonna go to the trailers," said Moose.

"I have to go back to the animals."

"C'mon," said Joe, with a wide grin. "Sleep with him."

Moose punched Joe in the upper arm.

"Ow, man." Joe rubbed the area. "That's gonna leave a bruise."

Moose said nothing as he walked up the hill to the parking area where the trailers were set up. Seagn split up from them, heading to the animals.

That's when she saw Shet standing under a lamp post.

"Shet?"

The small pony didn't move from the area as she approached slowly. She took him by the bridle and stared into his deep brown eyes. "What are you doing out here?"

She turned to the area where the animals were. All the gates were wide open.

"Oh, shit!"

She pulled Shet back to his pen. Bella was safely in her pen, asleep. The goats, sheep, and ram were gone. The pigs were found in the pen next to Bella. The feed bags and water jugs had been slit open by a knife, food and water mixing onto the ground.

She walked around the Midway, finding Bob, Mohawk, and another goat. No sign of the sheep or the other two goats.

Seagn stood in the middle of her area, turning around in a panic. *Who did this? Where were the animals? Were they stolen?* It was after two in the morning. Who could she call for help?

She saw a patrol car drive slowly by the carnival. An idea sparked.

She called 911.

•   •   •

The animal control officer showed up with the three sheep who had found their way into someone's yard and ate their petunias. Now the four goats were missing.

"They don't answer to their names," Seagn told the ACO and the two policemen that came with him. "They're rambunctious, so will probably run."

"It's okay," said the ACO. "They probably didn't get very far."

"You don't have any cameras set up, do you?" asked one of the police officers.

"The Post Office does," said the other, pointing across the street. "Maybe it caught something."

"I'll leave a message for Len to come down in the morning." The ACO ran his hand through his hair. "They shouldn't be hard to find. We don't get that many missing goats."

"I want to know who did this," Seagn stated. "I want them prosecuted."

Webby stormed by, looking like he had just rolled out of bed after sleeping in his clothes. His RV was parked where the trucks were, so he had to walk four or five blocks to the spot. "What the hell is going on?"

"Someone let your goats loose," said the ACO with a yawn, while the two cops separated and went back to their car.

"Not my goats." Webby tried to be intimidating with Seagn. "Where the hell were you?"

"Down the street. I only left them alone for a little while."

Said the ACO, "Probably some prank or the SPCA."

"I'm supposed to be inspected by the SPCA this weekend."

The ACO shrugged. "There's not much we can do tonight without the Post Office cameras."

"What about them?" Webby butted in.

"They might have caught who did this on tape. It depends on where the cameras were pointing."

Webby looked over at the building the post office was in, which had two mail trucks parked in the fenced-in lot.

"Sixteen," came a voice over the police radio that the ACO had on his shoulder.

The ACO clicked on the mic. "Go ahead."

"We found some goats running on the beach."

"Ten-four." The ACO nodded at Seagn. "I'll go get him."

"Do you want any help?"

"No, it's okay. Keep an eye out for the last goat. Maybe he'll come home."

"They're not that smart."

"Heh." The ACO went to his truck.

"That's great. That's just great." Webby waved his hands around the spot. "Somebody broke in and let your animals loose."

"I'm usually here at night, Webby."

"Now you got the cops involved. First rule, never get the cops involved."

"Why?"

"You just don't."

Seagn thought about Carlos and Shayna, and the rest of the workers. *They're not legal*, she thought suddenly, staring at Webby.

"What?"

"You hire illegal aliens."

"That's not true." Though he looked a little nervous.

"You're lying."

Webby drew himself to his full height, standing over Seagn. "You're not going to say a word about that. I don't need Immigration to come down on my ass when I have good workers."

Seagn was too tired to stand up to him. "Right. Whatever."

"Find those goats. I don't want to hear that they destroyed property. That's on you, not my insurance."

"I don't have insurance."

"Too bad for you, then." He turned away.

"You never said anything about insurance."

"Fatsy never had it, but then, he didn't do a lot of shit, it seems." Webby half-waddled his way back to the trailers.

By the time the animal control officer returned with two of the goats, Seagn was asleep on her feet and dawn was coming fast.

"I'm sorry I had them wake you up," she said to the ACO as she put the goats in the pen.

"More fun than trying to find the source of a barking dog."

Seagn chuckled.

"I'd get locks for those pens if I were you."

"On my to-do list."

The ACO nodded. "Going home to get some sleep."

"I can't now. I have to keep an eye out for Jack. I think we open at nine."

"Okay. Hope he comes back."

"Me too."

Seagn sat down in her chair. She didn't mean to fall asleep.

●   ●   ●

"*Baaaaaa!*"

"Come on, you stupid thing."

"*BAAAAAA!*"

Seagn bolted out of sleep to see Joe trying to drag a goat out of the pen.

"Hey!"

Joe froze.

"What're you doing?"

"Trying to get this damn goat in the fucking pen." He tugged on its neck, like a mother cat would do to her kittens.

Seagn rubbed her eyes, clearing her head. "Where did you find him?"

"Near the trailer this morning. Are you gonna help me?"

"Yeah, sorry. I passed out." Seagn got up, picked up the goat, while Joe held the gate open for her. "Where's Moose?"

"Getting breakfast, I guess. He was up before me. How'd the goat get out?"

"We don't know. Hey, I got a question."

"Shoot."

"Is Webby hiring illegal aliens?"

"Yeah, why?"

"Because I called the cops and he got all bent out of shape."

"Oh, honey," Joe said, closing the gate. "Never call the cops if it's something at the carnival. We handle it ourselves."

"What was I going to do, go to the trailers and wake you guys up?"

"Because of what?"

"The animals got out last night."

Joe frowned. "Yeah. Yeah, you'd wake us up and we'd go looking for them."

Seagn sat back down in her chair. "I wish someone would tell me all these unsaid rules."

"It's on a need-to-know basis."

"So break the rules and then get told about them?"

"That's how things go around here."

"Who makes the rules?"

"We all do. Webby sometimes has to step in."

"He's the arbitrator?"

Joe cocked his head.

"The one who decides things."

"Sometimes." He looked uncomfortable when he said it.

Seagn saw Moose crossing the street, carrying a large paper bag in his arms, and a coffee in both hands.

"Here comes your breakfast," said Joe. "I'll leave you two alone." He gave her a wink and headed toward the Midway.

Seagn got up and met Moose half-way.

"Tea," he said shaking his left hand. "Sugar is in the bag."

"You brought me breakfast? How sweet."

"You owe me twelve dollars."

Seagn took the bag. She could smell maple syrup and cinnamon. They walked back to the tent.

"Hope you like your eggs scrambled."

"I'll take them any way they come."

Moose laughed, then looked over at where the food bags had been torn open. "What happened?"

"Somebody let the animals loose last night while we were at the bar. I called the cops."

"Wha'd you do that for?"

"What else was I going to do?"

Moose looked at the goats, who were bleating for food. "I don't know. Does Webby know?"

"Oh, yeah."

He walked around the pens. "They all seem to be here."

"One of the goats was up at the trailer this morning. The rest were out and about getting into people's flowers and taking moonlit walks on the beach." She turned to see Webby carrying a nylon chair, walking from where the trailers were parked. Stephanie was behind him, carrying a cooler and another chair. "Speak of the devil and he appears."

Webby made a beeline toward Seagn. She put her breakfast on her chair, while Moose left to man his ride.

"You got all of 'em?" he demanded. Stephanie walked by them to the other side of the Midway.

"Yeah. All present and accounted for."

"Then we don't need the cops for nothin'."

"I want to know who did this."

"No, you don't."

"What?!"

"Leave it alone."

Seagn gave him a side-eye. "Do you know something about this?"

"I dunno nothin'."

"Where's Fatsy?"

"At The Ranch."

"I thought this was an all-hands weekend."

"I don't need Fatsy since I'm here. I'm not paying him for doin' nuthin'." Webby hitched the nylon chair higher on his shoulder. "Buy some locks." He went down the Midway to join his wife.

Seagn exhaled. She wanted to give him a sharp retort but chose instead to feed the animals begging for food.

Beau and Moose took turns guarding the flock while she walked to the nearest convenience store three blocks away from the beach. Highway robbery at $2 a gallon of water, she could only carry four gallons at a time, and even that was difficult.

Moose showed up with Beau toward twilight. Seagn was exhausted after constantly cleaning up the animal's messes — not to mention no sleep the night before.

"Come with me," Moose said, offering his hand.

"I have to stop at the bathroom."

"Of course you do." He took his hand back.

She waited in line for the portable bathrooms, wiping her hands with hand sanitizer when finished.

Moose offered his hand again.

Seagn stared at it, not sure what to do. What if she took his hand? Did that mean she would sleep with him?

"I don't want to lose you in the crowd."

She put her hand in his. His hand was large, callused, and engulfed hers. She entwined her fingers through his thick ones.

They walked together among the small groups of people gathered near the field. Leaving the carnival, they crossed the street to the beach and sat on the wall among other people. She could see the sun setting to their left. The western ocean reflected the sunset, with a pink and orange hued skyline, the clouds dark puffy cotton among the navy blue of the eastern sky.

She found herself leaning against Moose as they watched the colors grow darker. He wrapped his arms around her, and she sighed, feeling his body heat against hers.

He kissed her forehead, and she turned to face him.

He was gentle with the kiss that followed, betraying his size and strength, as if he was holding back. She found it refreshing that a man would be so sweet, so caring and attentive, not passionate and demanding.

Seagn pulled back from the kiss first.

Moose smiled. "Been wanting to do that for a while," he said.

She lay her head on his chest. "I know."

He didn't ask, "You too?" like she expected him to. He was so unlike the other men she had gone out with — not pushy, not wanting to get into her pants, but a kiss, a soft, gentle kiss, seemed to be all he really wanted.

The water now reflected the lights of the carnival. She didn't know how long they sat there, but she did notice people leaving one by one.

"We have to go back," she said.

"Yeah. Beau's probably wondering where we went off to."

He jumped off the wall, holding his hand out to her again to help her down. Seagn gave him her hand freely.

●　　　●　　　●

Seagn turned over in her sleep on the chair, knocking it over and sending herself cascading to the ground.

She jerked awake. Bella slept soundly in the dark with the goats next to her pen. Everyone slept, some snoring. It was still dark. She checked her phone for the time: 3:20 a.m.

Seagn straightened out her chair. She checked her phone, though out here there wasn't much of a signal for data. She checked her email anyway, even though it took upwards of a minute to download.

Nothing from Liam. Nothing from Anna saying Liam had shown up in Salem. Nothing from anyone at the clinic or the shelter. She was so alone.

Except for Moose.

She touched her lips with her fingertip. She still couldn't believe she kissed him. Or did she let him kiss her? She didn't know. It was all so sudden, in the moment. And it had been pleasant.

"He wasn't pushy," she said to a sleeping Bella. "It's all he wanted."

She smiled. Maybe she could go out with him after all.

Later, she woke up again to the sunrise. So did the animals, as they stirred and made noise to get her to move.

At seven, Moose appeared with another paper bag and two cups. "Got your tea with cream, two sugars. Careful, my breakfast is in there too."

"I owe you twelve dollars again?"

He paused, about to say something other than what he did say. "Yeah. Yeah, I think that would be the best thing."

She handed him fifteen. "Keep the change."

At least this time, the food was hot. She had been so caught up in feeding the animals the previous morning that she barely had enough time to eat her breakfast.

Moose sat on the cold, wet ground, while she sat in her chair. "How'd you sleep?"

"Woke myself up at three," she said. "Fell out of the chair."

"I didn't get to sleep until at least that."

"Went to the bar again?"

He chuckled. "With Joe, you always go to a bar."

"Is he an alcoholic?"

"He'd say he's recovering. So would Maggie."

"Recovering from what? He drinks like a fish."

"At night, after work. Not before, during, and after. That's why nobody will hire him. He was arrested on a DUI. He's got no license."

"He drives without a license?" *Yet another illegal*, she thought.

"He had a CDL a few years back, so Webby took him on to drive the Swinger's truck."

"Do you have a CDL?"

"Nope."

"You're not supposed to drive my trailer, either."

"Not by law. But I can drive it."

"Does everybody have something to hide here?"

"Yep." He sang, "*Gypsies, tramps, and thieves.*" He chuckled and gathered the trash. "Going with Beau to make sure nobody fucked with the rides overnight."

"Thanks for breakfast. I'll see you later?"

"We got extra people for teardown, so I'll help you."

"Thanks."

They opened officially at ten and would close at eight. She noted in her phone and did online pick-up shopping at Home Depot to buy locks and chains.

In all the time, she worried — about Maisey and the SPCA's inspection. *Maybe Maisey is up at The Ranch.*

People dressed up for Sunday church came by her place and the carnival to examine things. One group came by handing out small pamphlets with God-fearing pictures and stories of people going to hell. She tossed hers in the trash with the animal shit.

One of the people who came by was the ACO with a pair of young boys. He was out of uniform and waved to Seagn in greeting.

"Everyone accounted for?" he asked.

"Yes," she said, as she opened the sheep's gate for the two boys to go in. "Any luck on the post office?"

"The camera was pointed down into the lot. We couldn't see anyone up here."

Seagn frowned. "Damn."

"It was probably a college prank. They're not that far away from here." He turned to watch the two boys. "Are the sheep mad because they keep butting into the kids?"

"No. They're playing. They want to be petted." She let more kids into the goat's pen. She asked the kids, "Want to feed them?"

"Sure!" they responded.

She got a small bag and filled it with the feed. Instead of handfeeding them, the boys let the sheep eat out of the bag. The

ACO took pictures of the boys feeding the sheep. "For blackmail when they get older."

Seagn took the bags from the boys when they were finished.

The ACO patted one boy on the head. "Okay, let's go on the Tilt-A-Whirl."

"Can we go on the bumper cars?" asked one of the boys.

"We'll see." The ACO nodded to Seagn. "Thanks."

"No, thank you for helping me. Have fun guys!"

The rest of the day passed with nothing spectacular. Nobody got bitten; all the rides were intact; and sunset came with more pretty lights in the east.

Seagn smiled, thinking of the prior day's sunset, ending with a kiss. She turned toward Moose's ride to see him watching her. He waved with a smile to her.

13

"Good morning, sunshine," Moose said as he arrived to help pack the fencing in the trailer.

"Yeah, yeah," Seagn replied, trying to lift the fencing onto the trailer. The animals had already been herded into their pens, so now it was the fencing, tent, and lights that had to come down.

Moose helped her with the fence. "You're paying me for this, right?"

Seagn moaned. "Can we discuss payment after we pack up? I need sleep."

"Don't we all. There's something helpful called cocaine, you know."

She stared at him.

"No, not me. But I know where you can get some."

"No. No drugs."

"I don't either. Red Bull is as strong as I'll go. Remember how they reacted to knowing you had drugs? It's not only downers they look for; it's uppers, too."

Seagn silently watched Moose near effortlessly take in the generator. She brought out the ladder for him to bring in the lights.

In an hour, everything was packed. The last ride to leave was the carousel, when everyone, including Seagn, pitched in to take that down. She gathered the greasy three-inch screws that held the horses on their tracks. She didn't know until then that the carousel was always the last ride to get packed away and the last ride in the convoy.

She climbed into the cab with a heavy sigh. She glanced around for Maisey, but, of course, she wasn't there.

"Take a nap," said Moose. "We'll stop on the way home and I'll get a Red Bull."

"Too tired to take a nap," she said, closing her eyes and resting her head against the window.

"Too tired?" He laughed. "Wish I could say that."

"I just want to pass out."

"Go ahead. You've done it before."

"I'm sorry I'm not better company."

He turned up the radio. "This is."

•   •   •

Back at The Ranch, Maggie greeted them. Seagn just gave her a glare and headed to her trailer.

"What's with her?" she heard Maggie say.

"She's tired," said Moose.

"We all are," Joe stated.

Then Seagn tuned them all out.

She stood at the edge of the forest calling for Maisey, but no cat showed up. She put out tuna, her favorite, after she set up the fencing for the animals. Tomorrow, Tuesday, she was going to Home Depot and pick up the locks and chains. Also, she planned on heading to the Warwick Animal Shelter to see for herself if Maisey showed up there.

Her phone beeped when a new text came in. Not about Maisey, but Liam. *I'm at your place. Who do I see?*

Anna's shop wouldn't be open until noon, and it was 7:30 in the morning. She texted him Anna's personal number, with the caveat that she might be grumpy. Meanwhile she texted Anna a heads-up.

Once the animals were set up, she slept soundly in the truck's cab for six hours before getting up to eat an early dinner and feed the animals. When she finished, she saw Beau near her small truck, walking around it as if looking for something. He tried the passenger's side window, pulling down on it in an attempt to open it.

She stood and watched, her hand on her hip. "Beau?"

He froze and turned around. "Oh, *mon cher—*"

"Don't give me that French bullshit. Were you trying to break into my truck?"

He hunched his shoulders and looked down at the ground. "I — only wanted to … borrow it."

"You could ask me to take you somewhere."

"Not to Canada."

"To where in Canada?"

"Quebec. Back home. I have enough money now to go home." He raised his head and smiled widely.

"So, you would steal my truck and go to Canada? You wouldn't get very far."

"I know where there are some border crossings that have no police. I would cross there to Montreal and take a bus."

Seagn frowned and exhaled. "How long is it to drive to Montreal?"

He shrugged. "I don't know. And I have no papers."

She checked her phone. It was a five-hour drive. She checked where they could cross without an inspection.

"Whatcha doin'?" asked Moose coming over as was his new usual every morning.

"Helping Beau. He said he can go home."

"Is that right? Where's home?"

"Near Three Rivers," Beau said, almost breathlessly. "If I can get to Montreal, I can get home."

"Can you bring him?"

"A ten-hour drive?"

"I'll go with you. I've never been to Canada." He looked at Beau. "How much you gonna pay her?"

"I … I don't know."

Seagn and Beau shared a look. He wasn't going to pay her. He was going to steal her truck and pay for gas all the way to Canada, then probably ditch the truck near the border and get a bus to Three Rivers.

"Pay for the gas on the way up."

Her phone went off again. *In your apartment.* A picture followed of her living room, just the way she had left it.

Be careful, she texted back. Her passport was back home as well. But she had her veterinary license and other papers to prove she was a citizen. She doubted Moose had any papers on him other than his driver's license. *Did he even have a driver's license?*

"Are you certain?" Beau was saying while she texted.

"We'll go tomorrow. We should be back in time for set-up this weekend."

"You're not going," said Moose. "Some church festival. Four rides. That's it."

"No food trucks or gambling?"

"Nope."

"Will you be going?"

"Yeah, I have to go."

Beau said, "I will drive the way up. I know where I'm going."

"All right." Seagn sighed. "Let's get go now."

•　　•　　•

They left at almost eleven, stopping on the way for gas and lunch. According to the GPS on her phone, it should take just under five hours.

The radio picked up some mediocre stations as Beau drove northward. She tried to follow along with her GPS, but he went down back roads and route numbers she'd never even heard of.

"Are you sure you know where you're going?" she asked.

"I've been this way before," he said. "Coming to the States."

Moose smoked, but blew it out the window. Seagn found herself in the back seat, sitting sideways across the cushions.

"Been here often?" Moose asked.

"A couple of times."

"Who's back home?" Seagn asked.

"My parents and my sister. Little sister, Suzanne."

"Why did you come south?"

"There were no jobs where I lived. I wanted to do something no one in my family had ever done."

"Wanderlust," said Segan.

Beau smiled. "Yes, yes, that. Doesn't every child want to run away and join the circus?"

"A carnival and a circus ain't quite the same," said Moose. "There's more animals in a circus. Bigger tents. Nicer hotels."

"I wouldn't know about that."

After two hours in the back seat, Seagn's legs fell asleep. When they pulled over for some gas, Seagn had to drag herself out of the back and let her legs dangle to get the blood flowing again. She shuffled toward the restrooms.

According to her GPS, they were going parallel to the highway, but taking lesser-known route numbers along the way. Although they avoided rush-hour traffic on the highway, that didn't mean that they avoided traffic entirely. Beau was careful, using signals to change lanes, staying around the speed limit. He avoided speed traps and let cars cut in front of him without saying a word.

It took them until after dark to reach the border in Derry, Vermont. Beau pulled the truck over into a small dirt parking area just before the border line painted in the road. There were no lights, no houses or buildings, just a stretch of road leading out into the dark.

Beau hesitated, then picked up his knapsack from the bed of the truck. "Thank you," he said.

"Are you sure you're going to be all right?" Seagn asked while Moose helped her get out of the truck.

"I will be all right." He kissed Seagn on both cheeks, and then tried to do the same to Moose.

"Dude." He stepped back with a disgusted look.

Beau looked out into the dark. He walked to the border and jumped over the white line in the street. Seagn expected Royal Mounties to show up out of the brush, or a flash of motion-detector lights to shine on him, but nothing of the sort happened. He disappeared into the dark.

"What's wanderlust?" Moose asked.

"When you get that itch to travel. And you don't fit in to regular society."

"Is that what I have?"

She climbed back into the driver's seat. "Maybe."

Moose got into the passenger's side. "Do you want to get a motel for the night?"

"Let me see if I can find a faster way home." She pulled out her phone.

"Can't you live without that thing?"

"It's my wallet and my phone."

"You really don't need one."

"Why? Because you don't have one?"

"I never found the need to be led on by a beeping phone every ten seconds."

"You might not want to be connected to the world, but I do."

He crossed his arms and looked out the window. "You live with rich toys. Try to simplify sometime."

Seagn pulled onto the highway. "I really don't have time to waste to be simple."

"Isn't that why you joined the carnival? To have something simple to do?"

"I joined the carnival to nurse those animals back to health."

"And now that they are?"

"They're there to show people what farm animals are like. You need to see people when they see them. When they can touch them. It's like they're exotic animals that they've never seen. Especially the kids. It's great seeing kids play with the goats."

"So, it's like teaching them."

"Exposing them to something that they've only read about or seen on TV. Kids always read about farms."

"And this is what you want to do? Forever?"

"Not forever. A couple of years, maybe?"

"Then what?"

She shrugged. "No idea."

"I was thinking of doing this for a couple more years," Moose said. "Then try and settle down. I don't want to be 50 years old and still doing this for the rest of my life."

"I can't see doing this when I'm 50, either."

"Good thing we got a long time until then."

Seagn couldn't see herself at Ruby's age, living in a tent with her husband. In a momentary flash, she saw the other man she would be living with as Moose.

Seagn shook her head. She was tired of driving, no doubt. The highway was dark without lights at this time of night, so she only had the bobbing headlights of the truck and reflective paint of the lines on the road o guide her.

She pulled over into a 24-hour truck stop in the middle of Vermont. Both of them got out to stretch their legs.

"Excuse me," called a man walking toward the front of the truck. "I need money to get home."

"Yeah, right," said Moose, glaring at him. "You need it to buy drugs."

"No, man, I swear."

"Dude, I can tell."

The man turned to Seagn. "Just five bucks, lady. Enough to buy something to eat."

"Now you're looking for food?" Moose walked over to the front of the truck. "Make up your mind."

Seagn saw that the man was hallow-eyed, looking desperate. Seagn tucked her hand in her pocket, but Moose put his hand on her arm. "Let's go."

"C'mon, man. Just a buck. Anything."

"I can give —"

"Let's *go*." Moose pulled her arm, dragging her into the building. She didn't stop him until they got inside.

"If I gave him money, he would leave us alone."

Moose stood near a window, where he had a good view of the truck. "Go to the bathroom and do whatever. I'll be right here."

She did so, coming out of the rest room to see Moose still standing there.

"Watch the truck," he told her. "I'll be right back."

She was tempted to go outside and give the man some money, but Moose seemed adamant about it. She watched as the man paced back and forth in front of her truck, glancing her way once or twice before returning to pacing.

After going to the bathroom, Moose went to the clerk at the counter and said something to him. He only shrugged and cashed out the two Mountain Dew Extras Moose bought.

"Want anything?" he asked her.

"Let me get an iced tea."

Moose took up her position at the window. She found a can of Arizona peach tea and picked up one of those, in addition to some Combos. She had a couple of dollar bills in her hand. Not enough to buy anything else, but enough to get the guy off their back.

"Ready?" Moose asked. She nodded, and he opened the door for her.

As expected, the man whirled his whole body around to meet them on the pathway from the building to the parking lot. "Please, lady, enough to get some —"

She pressed two dollars into his hand. He brightened. "Thank you so much," he said with a broad smile.

"Come on," Moose said disgustedly.

The man followed them to the truck. "Would it be too much —"

Moose glared at him. Seagn could feel the "Don't Fuck With Me" aura he generated, almost like a blast of hot air. The beggar felt it too because he backed away.

Moose climbed into the truck when Seagn unlocked it.

"You didn't have to scare him," she said, as she started the vehicle.

"He was going to ask us for a ride," he said. "And you would have given it to him."

"No, I wouldn't have."

"You gave him money for drugs."

"How do you know it was for drugs?"

"How do *you* know it wasn't?"

"Look at him. He looks like half the carnies. They always look for drugs, people like that."

"Well, excuse me if I'm not as worldly as you are."

"What's that supposed to mean?"

"You've been telling me all about how bad people are since I joined up with this carnival. Have you ever thought that maybe there's some good among people?"

"Look, Shaun." He turned to her. "You're a good person. I was a good person. Then I got caught in the wringer of getting used by people. Have you ever been used?"

"Yes. Everybody has at one time or another. But that doesn't mean everyone is going to use you." She glanced at him. "Do I?"

He paused for a drink of the soda. "No," he finally said. "No, you don't."

"So relax, for once."

"You're the only one I trust in this gang of thieves."

She whispered, "Me too."

She felt him take her hand that rested on the shifter. "Sure you don't want that hotel room?"

"You have to get back by tomorrow for set up."

"Today. It's just past midnight."

"Hurray, it's Wednesday." She sighed. "No. I don't want to go to a motel room."

He rubbed a finger along the back of her hand. "All right." He started to remove his hand, but she took it, entwined their fingers, and rested on the console between them.

After one more stop for gas, they arrived back at The Ranch around nine in the morning.

14

T HE FIRST OF JUNE WAS A RAINY SUNDAY, so Seagn was glad
she wasn't with the carnival in Fall River. The animals herded
miserably into the trailer and she sat with them, feeling as bad as
they did.

Maisey was gone. Seagn visited the Warwick Animal Shelter
on Saturday. No Maisey. She came home depressed. Now she had
cravings for chocolate cake, which was her go-to when she was
upset. She drove in the rain to a Dunkin' to get a hot chocolate,
but that didn't hit the spot. She checked her bank account and
was stunned at the small amount. She was in the triple digits.

Seagn counted her cash. She had just over two hundred
dollars in cash. She wasn't going to get money for this weekend,
so she had to live on what she had and the amount in the bank.
She hadn't gotten feed, either. No organics this week.

Moose and Joe had gone with the group to Fall River, so she
had no one to talk to. She emailed Liam, then texted him, but got no
response. She was dozing off out of boredom when her phone rang.

"Good afternoon, sweetheart," said Gray.

"Hey! How's it going?"

"We're bored. Not good riding weather. I thought I'd give you a call to see how you're doing."

"Nothing going on today. I'm back at the holding area."

"Where are you going to be next weekend?"

"Let me check the schedule." She checked her phone, bringing up. a picture of the schedule Steph had given her. "According to this, we'll be at the Cape Cod Scallop Fest in Bourne."

"Cool. We'll come visit with your animals. I know the girls would love to ride a real horse."

"He's a Shetland pony and hasn't been broken yet."

"Do they really eat apples whole?"

Seagn laughed. "Not this one. He's too small."

"We'll bring apples."

"Bella the cow eats apples too."

"No shit?"

"I think the goats can too. They eat anything."

"Baby goats?"

"No, grown up ones. But they're small and cute just the same. And we have pigs."

"Pink pigs?"

Seagn sat back against the fencing in the trailer. "No, a black one and a mottled one."

"Definitely apples. Yeah, we'll get some," Gray said.

"You don't have to."

"C'mon, we wanna feed them, too."

"They never say no to food."

"Cool. We'll see you next weekend."

"Great." She hung up and smiled at Bella, who was chewing and staring at her. "It'll be good to see them."

A little while later, there was a knock on the side of her trailer. "You got a call."

She didn't know the voice, didn't know who would be calling her, and how, since she had her own phone. "Who's that?"

"Mark. C'mon."

Mark. Ruby's significant other. Ruby was the only other person in the group who had a phone, she remembered. But who knew both Ruby and her?

Seagn got up from her chair. She saw Mark standing out in the rain, the gutter from the trailer beating right on him. She avoided the sheet of rain from the gutter and jumped down to the ground, right in a puddle.

"Good thing it's a warm rain," she said.

He shrugged and walked away. Seagn followed as he tromped through the wet grass as if it was a bright summer's day. He took a well-established path deep into the woods near where the RV parked. A section was cleared out, with a large blue tent and an actual wooden outhouse nearby. There was a small wooden shed at the bottom of a sloping area away from the tent. She stopped to look at the area, noting that this was what Ruby did with all the money she got from robbing people.

Ruby came out of the tent, holding an old flip phone out. "A buck a minute," she said.

"They haven't charged that much since before I was born. Didn't you ever hear of an unlimited plan?"

She took the phone back. "Can't find her."

"Wait —"

"Oh, here she is." Ruby grinned and gave her the phone.

"Who's this?" Seagn asked.

"Webby. What the fuck's this about an inspection? Some guys in suits came here for an inspection for you."

"Did they say where they were from?"

"SPCA."

"Yeah, I'm expecting them."

"Well, I sure as fuck wasn't. They'll be at the Scallopfest next weekend to inspect your animals. Did they get shots and shit?"

"Yeeeesssss …" she said, while Ruby was looking at her watch, timing her.

"A'right. They better be. Gimme Ruby."

Seagn handed the phone back to Ruby. "Five bucks," she said.

"That wasn't even a minute!"

"Five dollars minimum charge."

"Oh, for God's sake!" Seagn stuck a hand in her jeans and pulled out a five, throwing it on the ground.

Mark bent and picked it up while Ruby walked back into the tent, talking on the phone. Seagn stormed back to her trailer.

•   •   •

"I wonder how Beau is doing," Seagn said while she and Moose set up the tent.

"Who cares," said Moose, tying the rope onto the stake. "He's got some balls leaving in the middle of the season."

Seagn swallowed. "I thought you would be happy for him."

Moose shrugged. "He wasn't getting all his drugs here."

"All what drugs?"

"Heroin. Weed. Downers." He straightened up from the stake. "He was trying to break in your truck to get your drugs."

"How do you know that?"

"Because he kept trying to sneak away from me the whole trip, to get alone with your truck."

"He didn't do a good job of it."

"Junkies ain't all that smart." He brushed his hands on his jeans. "'specially when they're looking for a fix."

Seagn pondered that as he moved to the next stake in the ground. "Is Ruby a drug dealer?"

"I wouldn't be surprised."

She followed him to the other stake. "Is everybody a junkie or an alcoholic?"

"I'm not." He shrugged. "I might smoke the Devil's Grass if I'm offered, but I don't go looking for it."

"Why?"

"Because I see what it does to people — it makes 'em desperate."

She also pondered how different he was from the carnies, and men in general. How on the outside he was tough as nails, but caught alone, in an intimate setting, how gentle he was.

"You okay?" he asked, as he straightened up.

"Sorry. Daydreaming."

"We still have to put up the fencing. Did you get the locks this time?"

"I got the locks and chains, yes."

"We can bring them in at night because we don't have to park the trailer away from the spot, thank God." He slip-knot tied another end of the tent to a spike.

"I'll do that instead of locking things up. It looks bad if I have locks."

"You got the SPCA coming in this weekend?"

"That's what Webby told me. I haven't spoken to him since that five-dollar phone call."

"You'll do fine. You have all their shots now."

Seagn nodded as they went to the trailer to get the fencing.

•   •   •

Someone banging on the truck door woke Seagn up. "What?" she yelled, pulling the sheet over her head.

"Someone out here to see you," called Moose.

She checked her phone. *Six thirty, for God's sake.* "It better not be Webby," she muttered. "Or I'll be very pissed."

She pulled on clothes and opened the door. Moose stood at the base of the truck, and beyond him …

"Gray!"

She jumped down and the older woman hugged Seagn, giving her a kiss on the cheek. Most of the group waved with a smile at her. Others looked like they needed a cup of coffee before becoming human.

"Morning, sweetheart." She thumbed at Moose. "Nice fella you got here. Appreciates good bikes."

"I have a riceburner back at the Ranch," he said.

Gray seemed to ignore him for the moment. She turned to Seagn. "We're here to take you for breakfast."

"Sounds like a great idea. We don't open until ten."

Sheila came forward. "Where's the animals?"

"In the trailer. I have to feed them first."

"We can help!"

Some of the women groaned. Gray waved a hand. "You don't have to if you don't want to. Why don't you scope out a place that can take us all."

"Mind if Moose comes?" Seagn asked.

"If he doesn't mind being the girl."

Moose shook his head. "I'm all right. There's a Denny's twenty minutes down Route 6 heading east."

"Denny's it is. The mom and pops won't be able to take us all at once. Shaun, you can ride with me."

Seagn stared at the bike. She gulped. "Do I have to?"

"Don't tell me you're scared."

Moose said, "Then I'll tell you. I've been trying to get her on the back of my bike for months."

Gray laughed. "I'll put a sissy bar on it. Katie? Can I borrow yours?"

"Sure, boss," said a young woman with long blond hair and a squat body. She took out an electric screwdriver she had in her saddle bags and unscrewed the metal bar at the rear of her bike.

"So you mean to tell me that the only thing that's going to be holding me on is a pair of screws?"

"And someone who's been riding Softails longer than you've been alive."

"What about the animals?"

"I'll feed them," Moose said. "We can all talk shop when you get back."

"Don't feed them too much. I don't have a lot left and we're going to be selling bags of feed. Check the water and bring out the troughs, and —"

Moose gave her a look. She felt that aura come up again.

"Yeah, just feed them."

"Okay," he said, and headed to the trailer doors. The animals, hearing the commotion outside, were now awake and demanding.

"A cow!" cried Sheila, after hearing Bella moo. "You have a cow!"

"Later, girls, later," said Gray. "Taurus is ready to tear off heads because we left without her coffee."

Someone provided Seagn with a helmet. She looked confused until someone showed her how to put it on and switched on the microphone for her. They were on CB channel 22. Nobody used CB radio except truckers and enthusiasts, so the channel was clear. Seagn got a jacket and then climbed on the back of Gray's bike, glad that it had a bar in the back she could lean against.

The gang of bikers all started up at roughly the same time, creating a roar that would have woken up anyone else in the area. They pulled out onto Route 6, heading east.

"So what's this festival for?" asked Gray, her voice coming in loud and clear on her speaker.

Seagn replied, "Different restaurants showcasing their famous scallop dishes."

"Scallop au gratin," said someone into her speaker.

"Scallop marinara," came another voice.

"Eww."

"It's just scallops in a red sauce over linguine."

"Sounds too gross to me."

"We're going to stick around," said Gray. "I love scallops."

The group started talking scallops, then seafood, then fish. None of it was of any interest to Seagn as holding on for dear life was her only focus for the moment.

They pulled into the Denny's parking lot, engines roaring, making people look in their direction. Seagn wasn't sure if she was happy or concerned that she was being stared at. Gray had ridden at the speed limit, but that didn't make her feel any better.

She got off the bike, shaking, struggling with the helmet, feeling claustrophobic and sealed in tight in the helmet. A woman undid it and she gasped.

"Takes some getting used to," said Gray. "Helmets give us blind spots, but there's laws in a lot of states, so we wear them by default. Plus, you can't hear anything once these monsters are let loose."

Seagn nodded after getting her footing and her courage back. She was thinking about the ride back. There would be more traffic. It would be a lot busier.

Gray put her arm around her shoulder. "It's not that bad."

"I've been brought up that these are death machines."

"Not if you know what you're doing and aren't cocky. You have to have respect for them. I have no respect for people who ride those speed bikes. Your friend, though, I have respect for him, even if he rides a rice-burner."

"He'd be happy to hear you say that," said Seagn, as they walked up to the front doors.

Twenty-two women in leathers, tanks, jeans, and jackboots all stepped into the empty Denny's restaurant. Seagn was underdressed in a windbreaker and a t-shirt, jeans, and sneakers. Gray stopped at the podium and waited.

"Don't be giving us a hard time," she said loud enough for people in the back to hear. "Or you'll be losing some good tips."

A light brown skinned waitress came out. "How many?"

"Twenty-three."

She looked around the corner in the empty section of the restaurant. "Give me a sec." She went there, rearranged a couple of tables of eight, and one for seven.

Gray smiled at her as she guided the women to their seats. "Your name, sweetheart?"

"Joy," the woman responded.

"A very pretty name."

Joy smiled. "Thanks. I'll give you a few minutes."

Gray took a seat that oversaw all the other women. Seagn sat to her left and another woman sat to her right. "Anything on the menu," Gray said.

"Coffee," muttered Taurus.

"Of course, coffee. Carafes even." Gray turned to Seagn.

"I drink tea," Seagn said.

"Yo!" A woman held up her hand in a virtual high-five. "Me too!"

Seagn held up her hand in respose.

Sheila said, "You both like getting the little teapots. Makes y'all feel special."

Seagn placed her order and the women chattered about the weather, the ride from P-Town (Seagn wasn't sure what that was), and eventually assholes of the road. Seagn kept quiet throughout, thinking about getting back on that machine. Would she throw up after getting off the bike?

"Penny for your thoughts, sweetheart?" Gray put her fork down.

"The bike. I'm afraid of the bike."

"I'll take it even slower."

"I want to get back as soon as I can."

Gray patted her hand. "You need to get over your fear, or it'll get the best of you. Sheila here, she was worried about getting her own bike, but now that she rides on her own, she'd never go back. Right, Sheila?"

Sheila looked up from her food. She was called, but she didn't know the question, Seagn could tell. Sheila smiled and gave them a thumbs-up.

A dictator does that, Seagn thought. Gray had these women wrapped around her gloved hand. That scared her more than the ride back.

What did I get myself involved with?

• • •

Seagn held onto Gray's waist with a death grip. Her stomach settled when she got within sight of the carnival.

Moose had done more than just feed the animals. He groomed them as well. "I would have put them out, but I don't know how you have this set up," he said when Seagn dismounted.

Seagn's heart swelled suddenly. She blinked at the feeling.

"Mind if we park behind your trailer?" Gray asked.

"Don't see why not."

"Parking's a premium at these things." Gray motioned everyone to the area behind the trailer. All twenty of them fit there, parked like dominos, so close they looked like a stiff wind would topple them all over.

Seagn led out the animals. Some of the Sidewinders guided them to pens. They loved the goats — just like everyone did — and hand-fed some of them while Seagn made up the feed bags for the kids. Some of the other women looked bored while the younger ones played with the animals before the official opening.

As soon as the music started for the carousel, it meant the carnival was open. A few minutes after ten, people started streaming in. The Sidewinders headed out into the carnival to check out the rides and wares.

Seagn watched as men of all types gathered near the bikes to look them over. "Harleys do that," Taurus said flatly to Seagn.

"You're not with everyone else?"

"Seen one carnival, seen 'em all. I don't like to leave the bikes alone." She yelled at someone, "Hey, don't touch."

The three men gathered around jumped back as if whipped. Taurus only chuckled as the men walked away. "See how easy it is?"

"Easy what is?"

"Train men. All you need is a loud commanding voice and they fall right into line."

Seagn didn't think Moose would obey that easily. Maybe after some time had gone by, she wouldn't necessarily "train" him, but they would respect each other. In her opinion, that's what it came down to: respect.

She realized what she was thinking. About Moose. About staying with him.

But what about the animals?

And Moose's attitude when Beau left the company — she knew she wouldn't be able to get him to leave now. Maybe when the season was done. She'd approach him.

Later. Sometime …

"Hey, lady," a man in an apron called to her. "You own these things?"

"These 'things' are farm animals."

"How much for the goat there?" He pointed at Bob.

"It's a ram, and he's not for sale. None of them are."

"You sure?"

She looked him up and down, figuring that he was a cook from one of the restaurants who had entered the competition. Maybe he was planning on adding Bob to his scallop dish.

"Definitely sure." She'd have to lock the animals in the trailer at night. She didn't trust the guy as he walked away.

She talked to Taurus during the day. In the conversation, she found out Taurus was called that instead of "Bull", which was too male for her. She didn't hate men, she just didn't find a need for them, even as sexual partners. That was all that Taurus would disclose about herself — not where she was from, who she was with, or why she joined the Sidewinders in the first place. She wouldn't espouse about Gray and her iron control over the group; she said nothing bad about the gang.

It bothered Seagn, that nothing bad was with the Sidewinders. They couldn't to be nomadic all the time. Where did they get the money to drive around? Did they have real jobs during the winter and did this during the summer?

Gray returned with the gang about an hour after the taste-testing and the food trucks were packing up. "Oh, my God, the winner so deserved it."

"What was it?"

She drank from a paper cup. Seagn could smell beer.

"Scallops with lemon and pepper over spaghetti. So fucking simple." She offered the cup to Seagn.

She shook her head. "On duty."

"For how much longer?"

She looked at her phone. "'til ten."

"We'll save you some."

"I don't usually drink —"

"Nonsense. We're gonna have a party."

Seagn should have said no immediately. Gray had a look in her eye that meant she wouldn't take no for an answer. Seagn looked away, toward the animals. "Need to get them ready to put them in the trailer."

"We'll be back in two hours with plenty of beer." She waved and headed into the carnival.

Taurus drank something from a flask before following Gray. "It's after five o'clock," she said. "I'm off-duty."

Things picked up after sunset. People crowded among the animals. Seagn had the kids hand-feed them until they were near bursting. Even the goats turned away from food. If she overfed them, they would be sleepy or, even worse, get sick all over some kid. Luckily, most of the kids started thinning out around nine, and what was left were drunken teenagers out for a night at the carnival.

"What the fuck kinda petting zoo is this," one of the kids screamed. Literally, she screamed as if Seagn was in the next town over.

"Calm down," said Seagn.

"Who the fuck'er you?"

"The owner."

"These are fuckin' lame."

"Thank you for the honest review. If you'd be kind enough to let them sleep off the food coma they're in —"

"I wanna pet 'em."

Seagn undid the latch for the gate. "Fine, but if they throw up on you, it's not my fault."

Unfortunately for her amusement, they didn't throw up. They barely moved. The girl kicked one of the goats making him bleat.

"That's it. Out."

"I think it's dead."

"He's not dead. Get out."

The girl flipped her off. "Fuckin' lame."

Seagn came close to swearing at the girl and her cronies. They all gave her a nasty look and headed away from the carnival.

That's when Taurus separated from the shadows and followed them. "Hey, bitch," she yelled. The girl turned around. Taurus held something in her hand, pointing it at the girl.

"Oh, shit," Seagn whispered hoping it wasn't what she imagined it could be.

Taurus fired a shot at her.

The girl screamed again, this time in terror. She ducked her head and ran, screaming all the way.

"Are you crazy?" Seagn ran over to Taurus, who was putting the gun back in a shoulder holster. "You could have killed her!"

"I know what I'm doing."

Seagn expected people to stream out of the carnival to find out where the shot came from. Nothing of the sort happened. Among the noise of the carnival, a gunshot sounded like fireworks and didn't attract any attention. Taurus headed into the ruckus of the carnival without looking back.

Seagn waited, staring out into the night. Surely the girl would get police. Surely there would be a scene. But no.

First rule: don't get the police involved.

Bullshit. First rule: don't carry a gun!

The carnival died down about an hour after her section emptied out of people. The Sidewinders came out from the edge of one of the rides. With the carnival lights behind them, they looked like Amazons in leather jackets coming out to battle. Or party.

"Beer!" Gray held out a six pack of Budweiser to Seagn. "You got some catching up to do."

"I don't drink. I don't like beer much."

Said one girl, "Oh, hoity-toity likes Chardonnay?"

"I happen to like a good merlot."

Enough women rolled their eyes that made Seagn realize Gray was the only person who was holding them back from leaving. Gray liked her for a strange reason, and what Gray liked, everyone else was supposed to.

"I need to bring the animals in."

"We'll do it. Get to drinking, girl. You want merlot? We'll find one."

"I don't need alcohol —"

"Everyone needs a little bit of alcohol." Gray handed over a can. "Drink it."

The voice of command made Seagn think of Hailey, of Fatsy, of Webby, of Moose, and everyone else who told her what to do. She slapped the can away and it spilled all over the grass.

Silence, except for the noise of the dying carnival.

Taurus uttered, "Now that was a waste of good beer."

"I said no, and I mean it this time."

"I see. It's too bad because we were going to sit here and drink all night, sleep in your trailer, and head home bright and early Sunday morning." Gray advanced on Seagn. "You ruined that."

Seagn could smell the booze and weed coming off of her. "You're in no condition to drive."

"Then follow my plan."

"I don't need to be drunk."

"Fucking prim little pussy," a woman said, giving Seagn a shove. "I say fuck her and we party here anyway."

Gray shrugged at Seagn. "It seems, my dear sweetheart, that you have some guests for tonight. Too bad you can't enjoy it."

•   •   •

Seagn found herself knocking on the back of a truck that Moose was staying in. The Sidewinders had not stopped and were in the process of singing "Viva Las Vegas" for the seventh time.

Moose opened the door. "They're *your* friends."

"They're not my friends."

"You brought them here."

"They came here on their own! Stop blaming me!"

"Webby's going to blame you if they break out and cause any shit to the rides."

"What do I do? Call the police?"

Moose sighed. "Tell them, nicely, that you want them gone."

"But they're all drunk. They're in no condition to drive!"

"Then tell them, nicely, to keep it down. Some people are trying to sleep."

"*Viva! Viva! Las Vegas!*" The women's voices echoed from across the makeshift street.

"You're no help," Seagn snapped.

"I'm not going to put my head in the lion's den of a bunch of drunken bikers. They may be women, but you don't fuck with drunken bikers." Moose looked around. "Come inside here. You can stay with me."

"No han—"

He kissed her. She was surprised, but not angry. He deepened the kiss slowly, gently like he did when they were beside the water.

Seagn blushed. "Maybe a little."

•   •   •

"VIVA LAS VEGAS!"

Moose banged with a broom handle on the metal trailer for good measure. The animals bleated, snorted, mooed, and generally started to make a lot of noise. Seagn could hear moaning inside the trailer.

"Rise and shine, ladies. You've overstayed your welcome."

"Fuck you, pal —"

Someone else threw up. Seagn moaned, "Oh, man, not in my trailer!"

Gray stepped to the edge of the trailer. She was covered in hay and smelled like Bella. "Not very comfortable," she said. "Everyone to Denny's."

"I smell like a goddamn barn," said one woman.

"You smell like a still," said someone else.

Slowly, all the women filed out of the trailer. Moose stood by absently tapping a marching rhythm with the broom handle on the bumper of the trailer. "I need a shower," more than one said.

"Not going to Denny's like this," said Taurus. "We look like shit."

"Time to go," Moose said. "I don't care where you go, but you can't stay here."

A couple of women flipped him off. Most got on their bikes and started them up, wincing at the loud noise in the quiet of the Sunday morning. Gray led the women onto Route 6, heading west instead of east.

"She didn't even say goodbye," Seagn said as the last bike bled onto the road.

Moose put his arms around Seagn's shoulders. "After the season …"

"Yeah?"

He nuzzled against her neck, tickling her. "Maybe I can try wearing the monkey suit again."

"Shaun, what the fuck was all that!"

Seagn turned to see Webby waddling in her direction. "What the unholy fuck was that shit?"

"A lion's den," said Seagn, looking at Moose. She and Moose shared a chuckle.

"Don't do that shit ever again."

Seagn saluted. "Sir, yes, sir."

Webby blinked. "Eh, okay." Webby headed off in the direction of the food trucks.

Moose offered his arm. "Shall I buy you breakfast?"

"Let me get these animals fed."

"I'll help."

"They get half-rations because I'll be selling bags of feed for the kids."

As they were doling out the feed, someone knocked on the trailer walls. "Excuse me, Mr. Shaun Conway?"

"Miss," replied Seagn. *Sounds like a woman*, she thought.

"Oh, sorry." The voice followed along the side of the trailer. "I'm from the SPCA and have come to check on your farm display." When the person stepped around the corner, she was surprised to see a mousey man with glasses dressed in a suit and tie. He held out a card to Seagn.

"Henry Marshall," she read off the card, "Nice to meet you. I'm Shaun."

"If you don't mind my asking, how do you spell it? With a 'w'?"

"S-E-A-G-N."

He took out an old-fashioned pen and paper notebook and wrote it down. "Strange spelling."

"My mother told it was Gaelic. I think she made it up to confuse people."

"Right. Okay, let's get down to business."

She held up her phone. "Everything is in a spreadsheet. I can transfer the file to your phone or tablet."

Henry raised his hands. "As you can see, we haven't exactly advanced with technology, I'll just take a look at the records, if that's all right."

"Sure." Seagn asked the AI on her phone to open the spreadsheet.

He took the phone and walked around in the trailer, checking the animals physically and making notes in his book. He also took pictures of each one of them from different angles.

Moose stood next to Seagn as she crossed her arms and watched Henry work. He put a hand on her shoulder. "You'll be okay."

"This Shetland for pony rides?" Henry called.

"No, he's not broken yet." Seagn replied.

Henry nodded, made another note. When he returned to Seagn he said, "I noticed you don't have their ages."

"The last owner didn't see fit to give that information to me."

Henry closed his notebook. "You should have that information at hand."

"Do I pass?"

"They look healthy enough. The cages are kept clean, but they seem small for these animals."

"I only have a ten-foot space, and sometimes not even that."

"I would suggest selling some of the animals to get more space. The cow, for instance, takes up a lot of room."

She wondered if she could trade Shet for some feed at Bondgarden. The pigs were old and big and never got touched as people avoided them. She couldn't see getting rid of Bella, as she was the main reason she had bought this crazy side show.

"I'll take it under advisement," she replied to him.

"Then as far as I'm concerned, it's competent, but not exactly five-star material."

Seagn's mouth tightened. She forced a smile and said, "Thank you for your time. I have to put them out for display now."

"Of course. Have a good day." He turned away from the carnival, heading toward a green older model car parked nearby,

"You passed!" Moose kissed her gently on the cheek.

"Not exactly with flying colors."

"You have plenty of time to get them up to where you want them."

She had a whole season.

15

T HEIR NEXT SPOT WAS OUT IN THE MIDDLE of the boonies of West Springfield, Massachusetts. It looked like The Ranch — a large empty field — but this one was located at the base of a mountain. Seagn hoped there wouldn't be an avalanche or rockslide.

She had divested of the pigs to a no-kill shelter in Dublin, Maine. Shet was in talks with Bondgarden Farms. He was too old to be broken, Carl had said, and he couldn't be used for pulling because he was so small.

"Somebody's pet pony," Carl said. "I'll see if I can find someone." Seagn left it at that the previous Wednesday before they headed west.

On the ride there, Moose held Seagn's hand in a comfortable grip. Every once in a while, he would kiss her knuckles then return to driving.

This was too good to be true. A romantic man who treated those he cared about like treasures. He even brought her flowers from the field one morning with her cup of tea.

She still hadn't gotten his real name out of him, though.

Rockwell wasn't the only entertainment. So was another group, Blackstone Traveling Circus. This was a real circus, with animal acts and a three-ring tent that took up most of the meadow. Rides scattered haphazardly around it, like bits of paper caught in reeds. Seagn was relegated to the very back of the Midway, away from the rides and food trucks.

She was getting sick of being considered last. She was considered second-rate by the SPCA. She was falling hard for Moose. So she did something she had not done anywhere else.

She scanned the want ads online.

While in the middle of reading a job entry, Seagn heard a loud pop and a crash. She ran toward the sound, along with half of the other carnies from Rockwell.

Two people lay tangled in lighting and a ladder. One lay motionless; the other struggled to rise from beneath the ladder.

"Moose!"

Seagn fought her way through the crowd to help Moose get free of the metal ladder. Moose got the ladder away from the man on the ground. Seagn realized that it was Carlos. Two men tried to wake him, but he didn't move.

"What the fuck happened?" Webby yelled in his usual voice.

"He was plugging in the lights," said Moose pointing up at the electric pole near the entrance of the meadow. "I held the ladder. He hit something because next thing I know, the ladder fell on me."

"Fuck."

Carlos wasn't moving. Seagn pulled out her phone.

"Don't do it," yelled Webby.

"He could be dead!"

"You check. You're a doctor."

She stared down at Carlos' prone form. *I'm a veterinarian, not a doctor.* But she quickly tossed her phone to Moose as she dropped to her knees to perform CPR.

Moose caught the phone, stared at it for an instant, then dialed. "Emergency, need an ambulance at the Springfield fairgrounds. Someone got electrocuted."

"Gimme that fucking phone —"

Moose held it at arm's length and could hear the dispatcher say "… there in three minutes. Does he have a pulse?"

Seagn felt his wrist. She put on her clinical demeanor and examined him like she would examine an unconscious dog. "He's got a pulse," she announced. "Weak, but getting stronger."

Webby paced around the area, worse than when Seagn called the cops. "Fuck. An ambulance ride. Hospital ER. They're fuckin' gonna bleed me dry."

The ambulance bounded through the meadow as Seagn got up from Carlos. "He might have brain damage, thanks to you. If you let me call earlier, we could have caught him in time."

"I lost another guy."

"Make it two," said Moose. "I quit."

"You can't leave in the middle of a gig."

"Watch me."

"Oh, yeah? Well, you can take those fucking barn animals with you. You're done here!"

The EMTs jumped out of the ambulance and Moose directed them to Carlos' prone form. Seagn didn't register at first what Webby said. The EMTs got Carlos to moan before they put him on the gurney.

Webby clenched and unclenched his fists as they loaded him into the ambulance. "Now he's going to a hospital. I'm not paying for his stupidity."

Moose whirled on Webby so fast that the wind brushed her hair when he did. He gave Webby a sound punch in the face. It took four cops to pull him off.

"I'll sue your ass!" Webby held his nose, blood leaking between his fingers.

"You'll get nothing." Moose shook off the cops. "I'm all right."

"Get off this gig! All of you!"

The ambulance took off. Seagn watched Webby storm back to the RV, while Moose came to her side.

"Well. We're done, at least for this weekend."

"I'm done," said Seagn. "Does Shayna know?"

"She's back at The Ranch."

"Is Ruby there?"

"Probably."

"You have her number?"

"No. Webby does."

"Webby was more concerned about how much money he'd be responsible for than calling Shayna." She pointed to the fencing. "Let's pack up and, maybe by the time we get home, Webby would have told her. I'll give her a ride to the hospital if he's still there."

"What about the animals?"

She walked toward them. "I guess I have to make some calls."

•   •   •

They started driving during the evening hours. Seagn was glad Moose had a bit of difficulty night driving because he kept quiet, and she could think. They had the weekend to figure out what to do.

After they pulled into the Ranch, Shayna came running out of the woods to her. She burst into tears and threw herself at Seagn. She hugged her as Shayna kept repeating the same words in Spanish. Moose shrugged, not knowing the language, either.

"Is he dead?" Seagn asked.

"*Morte?*" Moose tried.

Shayna wailed.

"Find out from Ruby what's going on. She's got to know."

"Give me twenty bucks."

"I'm not paying her to tell me if Carlos is alive or dead! This has got to stop!"

She passed Shayna over to Moose, who awkwardly caught her. Then she marched to Ruby's tent — until it got too dark to see, then she stumbled her way there. She found her way by following a light in the woods.

"Ruby! Get up, you fucking bitch."

"What do you want?" She replied from inside the tent, not even bothering to come out.

"What happened to Carlos?"

"He's in the hospital."

"Which hospital?"

"I didn't ask. Tell that bitch she owes me five bucks for that phone call. Now go away."

Seagn had many select words for her, and almost used them. She walked back to the trailer, where she could see the lights through the trees. Shayna leaned against the Tacoma, wiping tears from her face.

Seagn used her phone to find that there were two hospitals in the area of West Springfield. She struggled to remember her first year of Spanish.

"We need his last name," she told Shayna, who looked confused as ever. "I can't call the hospital without a name. And even then it's sketchy because of the privacy laws."

"Have her call," said Moose.

Seagn pointed at her phone. "Hospital," she said.

"Hospital." Shayna nodded.

"You call them." She handed Shayna the phone. "Press this button."

She pressed the green button to connect the call. Thankfully, a voice came on in Spanish, and Shayna pressed the appropriate number. When someone answered, she asked for him, Carlos Sanchez. She waited, saying "Gracias" before hanging up. She shook her head.

They found him at the second hospital, the one in Westfield. Shayna said something in Spanish and hung up.

"It should take us a couple of hours to get there. They should be done with him by then."

Moose said, "I'll take care of the farm. You take her down there and back."

It was after two o-clock on Friday morning by the time she got on the highway with Shayna in the passenger seat. The radio faded in and out, so she used her phone to play music to keep herself awake.

They arrived at 4:30 a.m. and saw Carlos sitting on a bench outside. Shayna ran up to him and hugged him. Seagn let them have their precious moment before butting in.

"Excuse me, but I haven't slept. Can we leave?"

Carlos nodded. "Can you bring me to the gig?"

"You want to go back there? Webby swore up and down that he wasn't responsible for you —"

"We need the job, Shaun. I have no papers."

Seagn looked down. "We quit," she said. "Moose and me."

"You can find a job anywhere. Moose is a citizen. He can get a job, doing anything. Not us. We can't live here. We can't work a good paying job here, either."

Seagn looked up at them. Shayna held onto Carlos as if he would float away. And he very well could if Immigration knew.

"I'll bring you to the gig."

He said something in Spanish to Shayna. "Shayna will stay with me from now on. Maybe she can do some work."

Seagn climbed into the truck.

It was dawn when she dropped them off at the gig. She couldn't drive anymore, so she pulled into a Wal-mart parking lot and took a catnap for four hours.

•   •   •

When Seagn crawled onto The Ranch, Moose was at the campfire. She parked the truck and leaned against the seat, watching Moose amble his way toward her. He seemed to force himself to move slowly so as to not look desperate.

He leaned into the open passenger-side window. "I was worried sick."

"Sorry. I was too tired."

"First thing I'm getting when I get a real job is a phone."

"What kind of real job are you gunning for?"

He shrugged. "I can do general day labor to start until something opens up. What about you?"

Seagn looked to the trailer. "I have to call Bondgarden Farms. See if they'll take the animals in exchange for a free Tacoma and a half-years' worth of free vet services."

"We can sell the rig to someone, and the trailer for scrap. Where are you going to live?"

"I've got a few of months on my lease in Salem. Then, who knows. Maybe I'll move south."

"I hear North Carolina is pretty."

She laughed. "Not really south."

He brushed back long hair from his face. "Would I be imposing —"

"My brother is crashing there until the fall semester starts."

"Oh, then, I guess I can —"

"We'd have to sleep in the same bed."

His hazel eyes twinkled. "I wouldn't mind that."

"One thing." She looked sideways at him. "Your real name."

He grinned. "I'm named after a duck." He nodded toward her ever-present phone. "Use that to figure it out."

ABOUT THE AUTHOR

Lisa Jacob has been writing since she could hold a pencil and draw a straight line. She wrote fan fiction before branching out into novels and short stories.

In the early 2000's, Lisa was a carny in a traveling circus for a summer, where she met her husband. Interested in magic(k), cards, and divination, she lives in Rhode Island with her son and three cats.

Lisa is also the author of the "Grimaulkin" and "War Mage" fantasy series, as well as *Real Magic for Writers*.

You can find out more about Lisa Jacob at her website, *lajacob.com*.

ALSO BY LISA JACOB

GRIMAULKIN

Book One in the "Grimaulkin" Series

by L. A. Jacob

Treading the straight and narrow is not natural to one who summons demons.

WAR MAGE

Book One in the "War Mage" Series

by Jake Logan and L. A. Jacob

In war, here be dragons.

Available from Water Dragon Publishing in
hardcover, trade paperback, and digital editions
waterdragonpublishing.com

REAL MAGIC FOR WRITERS
by Lisa Jacob

Magic is real. Magic helps in everyday life.

It also helps with writing.

Available from Unruly Voices in
trade paperback and digital editions
unrulyvoices.com